# BLAZE

## THE FIREFIGHTERS OF DARLING BAY 1

### RACHAEL HERRON

Hga

# ALSO BY RACHAEL HERRON

## Cypress Hollow Yarns

Abigail's Shop

Lucy's Kiss

Naomi's Wish

Cora's Heart

Fiona's Flame

Eliza's Home

## The Songbirds of Darling Bay

The Darling Songbirds

The Songbird's Call

The Songbird Sisters

## The Firefighters of Darling Bay

Blaze

Burn

Flame

Heat

## The Ballard Brothers of Darling Bay

On the Market

Build it Strong

Rock the Boat

### Darling Bay Short Stories

A Darling Bay Christmas: Three Heartwarming Holiday Short Stories

Honeymooning: A Cypress Hollow Yarn Short Story

### Women's Fiction Novels

The Ones Who Matter Most

Splinters of Light

Pack Up the Moon

### Memoir

A Life in Stitches: Knitting My Way Through Love, Loss, and Laughter - Tenth Anniversary Edition

Unstuck: An Audacious Hunt for Home and Happiness

### Nonfiction

Fast-Draft Your Memoir: Write Your Life Story in 45 Hours

Fast-Draft Your Memoir: The Workbook

Letters to New Authors: 29 Encouraging Letters to Your Inner Writer

### Thrillers (as R. H. Herron)

Stolen Things

Hush Little Baby

# CONTENTS

Publisher's Note: This is a work of fiction. Names, characters, places, and incidents are a product of the author's imagination. Locales and public names are sometimes used for atmospheric purposes. Any resemblance to actual people, living or dead, or to businesses, companies, events, institutions, or locales is completely coincidental.

Blaze / Rachael Herron. — 2nd edition

HGA Publishing

Copyright © 2014, 2024 Rachael Herron

All rights reserved.

ISBN-13: 978-1-940785-75-2

*To my main squeeze, for always putting the whoop in my
siren.*

# CHAPTER 1

Everything was fine until the air conditioner caught on fire.

"It's not a big deal," said Grace, blowing at the tendril of smoke that rose from the plastic cover. "Don't get up."

Steve Swanson, who had been reclining with his needles in, popped his chair forward. His eyes bulged behind his thick glasses. "Kind of looks like a big deal to me."

Mrs. Little—who was anything but—also sat forward, adjusting her bosom as she went. "It smells like my toaster when the bread gets stuck. You sure it's not on fire in there?"

Eliza Cross, ninety years old if a day, didn't even open her eyes. "Just let me know if we need to evacuate. Till then, I'm napping." The *hush* was implied in the retired librarian's tone.

Grace waved her hands at the smoke. "I think it's dissipating," she said hopefully. No, this wouldn't do, not at all. A fire in her group acupuncture treatment room wouldn't be the best thing for business. Darling Bay was as progressive as small towns got, but residents were still figuring out what community acupuncture *was*. Word of patients being treated for smoke inhalation would be downright embarrassing.

The innards of the air-conditioner gave a startling crack followed by pops, as if something were being cooked inside. A larger cloud of noxious-smelling black smoke curled into the room.

"Oh, dear," said Mrs. Little. "Should I take my needles out?"

"No, no, let me ..." said Grace. "Just one sec. I think I can ..." She tugged on the front of the unit, pulling hard until the cover came off in her hands. When she peered into it, she saw a bright red flame leap. "Oh, crap." What were you supposed to do for an electrical fire? Baking soda? This was an office, not a kitchen.

"Get a jug of water!" said Steve.

"Not water." Grace remembered that, at least. "I've changed my mind," she went on briskly, clapping her hands. "I think the three of you should wait on the lawn. Eliza, let me help you. You can leave your points in—it won't hurt them to move around a bit." She kept her voice as even as she could, but inside, she was terrified. What if her whole office burned down because she waited too long to call the fire department? Her fingers shook as she dialed 911. Fire insurance was good from the day she purchased it, right?

Lexie answered.

"It's me, Grace."

"You usually text me. Why are you calling me at work?"

"Um, I might have a fire."

Grace heard Lexie sigh, and the clicking of a keyboard on the other side of the phone. "What's on fire?" She gave Lexie the information as fast as she could. The fire was getting bigger, flames licking out the top of the unit now. The metal Venetian blinds were charring, and the cord started smoking.

"We're on the way," said Lexie. "Can you get everyone out?"

"I'm trying." Grace ushered her three patients out, shooing them like chickens. Their acupuncture points bobbed, swaying lightly in their arms, legs and ears.

Steve, on his way out the front door with his pants still rolled up to the knee, said, "Aren't you supposed to have a fire extinguisher?"

Of course she did! How could she have forgotten? Demonstrating she knew how to use it was one of the check-offs she'd done for the city before getting her business license.

Grace made sure Eliza was comfortable on the lawn (the old woman was remarkably unperturbed and appeared as if she might go back to sleep) and then rushed back inside. The air was acrid, smelling of melted plastic and something harsher, more chemical. Grace felt dizzy and wondered if it was possible to pass out from smoke inhalation when it wasn't a *real* fire. It wasn't, after all, like a wall was on fire. Yet. She was pretty sure it was still contained to the unit. Mostly. Hopefully.

She got the fire extinguisher off the wall, finding it heavier than she remembered. Would she have to read the instructions? The list of words on the fire extinguisher was discouragingly long. In the distance, she could hear a fire engine's siren. Although now that she had the extinguisher, she bet she could have it out by the time they got there. Grace knew one thing about herself—she was good at handling a crisis.

Well then, *crap*, why hadn't she thought to unplug the

danged air conditioner? Reaching forward, she yanked out the plug and threw open the window next to it. Fresh air, at least.

Or would that make the fire happier? Fire wanted oxygen, right? What if the fire sped up the wall into the attic? The cottage her office was housed in was more than a hundred years old. She'd barely glanced at the attic when she bought it, just noting it was dusty and had housed mice at some point over the years.

Speed. *Hurry.* Grace stood straight, willing herself to breathe slowly. She pulled the pin on the fire extinguisher and pressed the handle, directing the nozzle at the air conditioner. The fire inspector, when testing her business, had instructed, "Sweep the spray side to side, hitting the base of the fire."

The difference was instant. The fire that had been creeping up the wall disappeared in a blanket of white spray. Grace took a deep breath of relief and immediately convulsed in a fit of choking.

From behind her, she heard a man yell, "Got a victim here, roll medics code three!" She turned to see a huge man in some kind of a yellow jumpsuit coming at her. He had shaggy blond hair and a jaw like a cliff. His eyes snapped green fire at her. Or that's what it felt like.

She tried to tell him she wasn't hurt, that she had it all under control, but she just said, "Thhbt."

Then everything went dark.

## CHAPTER 2

The woman was coming to, and that was a good thing, because Tox needed to make it clear to her how stupid she'd been.

What he wasn't ready for, though, was the moment she opened her eyes. Eyes the color of coffee with a splash of cream, lids heavy, as if she'd just woken up in her own bed after a restful night. She gave the impression she woke up happy, half a smile on her face. What must that be like?

"Glad you're awake, Princess."

Behind him, Tox's engineer Coin laughed. "Or what? You were going to kiss her awake?"

Sudden color flooded the woman's cheeks, and Tox could almost see her remember what had happened.

"Is the fire out? Is everyone okay?" She looked around, and relief lit her face as she saw her three patients studying her with interest. "Is the building okay?"

"You're gonna need a new air conditioner," said Coin. "And part of a wall where we pulled it out."

Tox interrupted him. "That's really not what you need."

"What?" she asked. "More? Did it get into the roof? The attic?"

Tox shook his head. "There was no extension. You were lucky. But you *will* need to get a clue the next time something like that happens. You should *never* have gone back in there, not after you got everyone out."

She frowned. "But I put out the fire, right?"

Well, he had to give her that. "You didn't know how it would go. Fires double in size every thirty seconds, and if it had caught inside the wall, in the time it took us to drive from the station, it wouldn't have been safe for you to use the extinguisher. That's *our* job."

"Oh, it's your job, huh?" She blinked sleepily, looking up at him. Summer sunlight lit her long maple-colored hair and for a moment he was tempted to lean down and pick her up, moving her into the shade. Skin as porcelain as hers would burn in a second.

"Darn shootin', it is."

She coughed again. "So I did it wrong? The fire's still raging inside?"

He heard Coin snort behind him. But Tox was right about this. "Next time you have a fire—"

"There won't be a next time."

He ignored her. "Next time you have a fire, you let us handle it. You seriously could have killed yourself. We see it all the time."

She looked concerned. "Really?"

Not for years, actually. They had a good track record in Darling Bay. "Yep. How's your breathing?"

The woman waved her hand at him and pushed herself up to sitting. "Pfft. I'm fine. We Rowes don't break *that* easily."

Tox frowned. "Rowe. Related to Samantha?"

She nodded. "She's my younger sister. I'm Grace. You know her?"

Grace looked suspicious, and Tox could understand why. Back in the day, Samantha had been a wild one. "Hank, my firefighter in there, I think he used to date her."

She groaned. "In advance, I'm sorry for whatever he's about to say. She had a rough few years."

"Whoa, slow it down. I remember her. She was cool."

"For the record, she still is."

Tox nodded and checked the pulse-ox. "Your O2 sat's good. Just got to get a couple questions answered from you, then the medics will take you to the hospital to make sure you're all right."

After coughing again, Grace pushed herself to her feet. "No hospital."

Coin gave him the high sign and went back into the business. Tox sighed. He was a sucker. He always fell for it, and winded up being the one to argue with the patients who wanted to AMA out of the transport.

"Ma'am, we always recommend—"

"Ma'am? Really? I'm thirty-three."

Tox ground the pen he held against his palm. "Ms. Rowe, we always recommend that our patients see a doctor. They can give you the medical advice that out here in the field, we're not equipped to give."

She was a ball of energy, practically bouncing on her toes. "What do you think is wrong with me?"

"You inhaled superheated gas. Your lungs should be checked."

"My lungs are fine."

He tilted his head. If he had to argue with someone today, at least she was prettier than the normal octogenarians who called them. "You're probably dying."

Her mouth dropped open. "I bet you're not supposed to say that to your patients."

"Normally they're too deaf to hear me say it."

"Now you're being mean just for fun."

Tox felt his mouth twitch but he wouldn't allow the smile. "We should just take you to the hospital."

"No, thank you."

"You'll need to sign that you're not going, against our medical advice."

"Gimme a pen," she stated, reaching out her hand as if she were going to take the one he was writing with right out of his hand.

He closed his fingers tighter around it. "Look, I'm all for *not* transporting you. I'd like nothing more than to get back to the firehouse where Coin just finished burning the popcorn. We have the Maple-Bruns fight ready to go on the DVR. But I'm not kidding. You're lungs aren't something you want to mess around with."

"How much does the ride in your little lights-and-siren box cost?"

Tox raised a shoulder. "I don't send the bills, but your insurance should cover it."

"What if I didn't have insurance?"

Tox couldn't hide the surprise in his voice. "Huh. You seem like someone who'd be covered."

"What does that mean?"

"I mean you have all your teeth, and you're not obviously on meth. You appear to have good hygiene." She had very good hygiene, in fact. She smelled annoyingly sweet under the smoke, like flowers and soap and something he wanted to move toward. He didn't like the feeling.

The small smile that had almost started on her face disappeared. "So you're profiling your patients now?"

"Hard not to sometimes."

"Really. In Darling Bay? Huge crackhead problem here?"

"You should see the guys in the inland flats. Those guys have pit bulls for a reason."

"*Seriously?*"

She looked angry enough to spit hypodermic needles. He leaned against the light post. Peering over her head into her practice, he could see Coin and Hank were just about finished up inside. "You probably have a pit bull, too."

"No, but I have a sister who's had a problem with drugs, as well as a mother who lived in those inland flats. And I *like* pit bulls. You're kind of pushing all my buttons right now."

"Your mother's a crackhead?" He couldn't help it. It was too fun. Something about this girl was getting under his skin and he didn't know if he wanted to make her laugh or make her slap him.

"She's dead."

"Oh." Tox looked at his worn boots. "I'm sorry about that."

"She didn't have insurance. Pretty hard, taking care of a person dying of cancer when no doctor will return your calls. Some people have to prioritize eating," she said. There was a glossy sheen to those big brown eyes, but it didn't look like sadness to Tox. It looked more like fighting-mad. "Some people don't have the luxury of working a job where they get to sit around in recliners and watch TV all night, every night."

"Hey, now." The woman didn't need to start pushing *his* buttons.

"I've driven past the station. I can see that blue glow.

Must be nice to have a job where the taxpayers pay for your insurance. We little people have to buy our own."

Oh, now she'd done it. One of his least favorite topics. "I'm a taxpayer, too, you know. Everyone always forgets that. I'm paying my own wages—my own insurance—out of my own pocket."

"That's a ridiculous argument. And by the way, I asked you what would happen if I *didn't* have insurance. I do have it, in fact. I just choose to trust Eastern medicine more than the hospital you want to take me to."

Tox got out the paperwork. "Here. Fill in this top part, if you really don't want to get checked out. I still think you should. Sign here." He yelled at Bonnie Maddern on the ambulance, just pulling up, that they could cancel. Bonnie thumped the outside of her door in understanding.

Grace scribbled on the page, her handwriting furious and choppy. She looked up at him with those huge eyes. Her lashes curled and were so long they looked fake, though she didn't look as if she were wearing any other makeup.

"You know," she said, clicking the pen closed with a flourish, "I don't think you're representing your company very well, Mr. Whatever-Your-Name-Is."

"Department." Specificity mattered. "I'm not representing the Darling Bay Fire Department very well. And I'm Tox."

"I thought it was protect and serve."

Oh, he'd protect and serve her, all right. This time he felt his mouth quirk into the smile he was trying to prevent, and he couldn't—seriously, he *couldn't*—prevent his gaze from dropping to the top of her flower-printed blouse. "You know, it's not the first time I've ever heard that complaint."

"I'm not surprised." She spun on the heel of her ugly clog which should have decreased her attractiveness by a multiple of ten if Tox hadn't found himself suddenly strangely aroused by plain black leather. Leading in two of her patients, she shouldered her way past Coin, muttering something about smoke damage.

Coin shouldered his axe and said, "If she thinks *that's* smoke damage? My ex-wife did more damage frying blackened catfish than that little bit of smoke she's got in there."

Tox frowned. "You set up the blower?"

"Yeah, it didn't even take three minutes to send it out the back door. TIC's clear." Coin said, referencing the thermal imaging camera they used to make sure fire hadn't spread elsewhere in the building.

"She's not taking a ride with us."

Coin signaled Hank and headed across the grass toward the engine. "That's not smart. That cough sounded like something that should get checked. And she DFO'd."

"I know, right?"

"Ain't she some doctor? She should know better, right?" Coin swung himself up to the driver's seat.

"A doctor who does voodoo with needles?" Tox said. "Not likely."

"You know, Lexie in dispatch swears by that stuff." Behind them, Hank jumped on board. Coin started the engine. "Let's hit it."

"Hold up," said Tox.

"What?" said Coin, releasing the air brake.

"I just ... Wait, that's all. I'll just be a second."

Inside the clinic, the air still smelled faintly of burnt electrical wiring, but he barely noticed. Grace was yanking those tiny little needles out of the old guy's face. Tox winced.

She dropped the needles in a sharps container and

turned to face him. "Not done harassing me about being unable to afford health-care in this great state of ours?"

He shook his head. For reasons he couldn't explain, he handed her the albuterol inhaler he'd brought inside.

"What's this?"

"Use it if you feel short of breath. And seriously, if you have any pain at all, you have to go see someone. Lung infections aren't to be messed with."

Her eyes softened a little. "You gonna send me a bill for this, too?"

"No."

"Then, why ..."

Gruffly, he said, "Just use it if you have to. It'll make me feel better."

She gave a small quick smile. One that he wanted to see more of. "Well. Thank you. Now, if you don't mind, I have to see to Mrs. Little."

He raised his eyebrows in salute—it was really all he could manage. Something about Grace Rowe tangled his tongue and his brain-waves at the same time.

As he walked back toward the truck, he touched his side pocket. He'd have to remember to replace his inhaler with his extra when they got back to the station.

# CHAPTER 3

Grace groaned and rubbed her belly. Her sister Samantha had taken on many professions since she turned eighteen, from truck-stop waitress to exotic dancer, from well-driller to—astonishingly—legal secretary, but in Grace's estimation, the best job her sister had ever had was the stint she took as cook at a small diner in southern Tennessee a few years back. No one knew how to cook bacon crisper or fry chicken greasier. Nothing Samantha made was healthy, but that was something they were working on. Okay, that was something *Grace* was working on at least.

"That was amazing. What do you even call that?"

"Hush-puppy-corn-fritter-sausage casserole. Or as I say, Mash'n'Smash."

"You know this is Northern California, right? You could get arrested for that in seven counties."

Samantha's eyebrows jumped. "Really?"

Grace held up her hands. "Teasing. That's all." Crap. It wasn't ever smart to joke about arrests of any kind in front of Samantha. You'd think she'd remember once in a while. "It tastes amazing. I wonder how we could make it a little more heart-healthy?"

Samantha laughed and untied her apron. "I can tell you exactly—substitute spinach and quinoa for all the ingredients, and then curl up in a ball and weep from hunger pains." She cleared their plates from the table.

Grace stood, trying to grab one of the plates back. "No, for once, can I do the dishes in my own house?"

Samantha shook her head. "We talked about that. It's my job."

"This isn't your job. I *want* you to live here."

"I've always made my own way. You know that." Samantha looked at her hands as she ran the hot water into the sink. "If I could contribute, I'd feel better. If I could just find a dang *job*."

"What about that thing you were doing, editing college applications?"

"Pays next to nothing. And I swear they just write whatever I tell them to. But yeah, I do have a little money to give you."

"That's not what I meant."

"I know," said Samantha sharply. "It's what *I* meant."

Grace hated hearing the frustration in Samantha's voice. She would do anything to take it away. There was a time when, heartbreakingly, she hadn't been able to do a single thing to help her sister. Now that Sam was clean, now that she was trying so hard ... Grace wanted to fix everything for her, to make everything all right.

"Later," Grace said, shutting off the water.

"Why are you coughing like that?"

Grace cleared her throat. "I'm not. Come on."

"What are we doing?"

"Change into your workout clothes. We're going for a run."

Sam gave her a look of horror. "Are you out of your ever-lovin' mind? I will blow chunks from here to the harbor. Did you see what we just ate?"

"That's *exactly* why we're going for a run. I don't want us to die of a cardiovascular ... thingie anytime soon."

"We're too young."

"I know a woman who had a heart attack at thirty-four."

Sam crossed her arms in front of her and looked at her challengingly. "Who?"

Grace dried her hands and then wiped down the already-clean counter. "No one you know."

"Her name?"

"Um ... Okay, maybe I read it in a magazine."

"One of your holistic yogapuncture journals?"

"It can happen."

Samantha pulled a rubber band out of the junk drawer and pulled up her long, brown, gorgeous hair. No matter what, Sam's hair always looked amazing, thick and wavy, even just rolling right out of bed. Grace, on the other hand, knew that now, by the end of the day, her hair was wild in all the places it wasn't flat.

Handing a second rubber band to Grace, Sam said, "Fine. If by run you mean jog."

"Girl, I think I might mean walk fast." Grace patted her overly-full stomach again. "I have no more interest in losing my dinner than you do."

CHAPTER 4

It wasn't until they were fast-walking down Lowry Avenue on their way to the marina that Grace realized their walk would take them past the fire station. Part of her wanted nothing more than to pass in front and peer inside. Sometimes, when she'd walked by before, she'd noticed she could see the firefighters in the kitchen through a screened window. It looked so homey that once she'd stopped dead in her tracks, staring inside at the man at the stove, stirring a huge pot that had white steam billowing out of it. Another guy had stood at the center island chopping something she couldn't identify. A third man had been by the sink laughing while rock music filtered out.

Grace wondered now if one of them had been Tox.

Certainly it hadn't been the laughing one.

"Let's go down Clackman Street instead."

"Why?" Sam's ponytail swung. She was walking faster than Grace wanted to, which was a little galling.

"Change of pace."

"But I want to go past the fire station," said Samantha. "Maybe we'll see the guys working out."

"Exactly what I *don't* want to do," said Grace under her rather short breath.

"What's wrong with you? Are you wheezing?"

"I'm fine."

Sam put out a hand and slowed Grace down. "No, wait. You're not. You're flushed and your breathing sounds funny. Oh, jeez, are you having a heart attack?"

Grace leaned forward and put her hands on her thighs. Maybe she should have brought that inhaler Tox had given her. She hadn't even thought of it. "I'm not having a heart attack."

"You *are*. You totally are. I'm calling 911." She fished around in the front of her bra for her phone—that was another thing they didn't have in common—Sam had enough rack to hold a cell phone, whereas Grace couldn't have hidden a tissue in hers without it being obvious.

"Over my dead body will you call 911." Grace took a careful breath. It didn't hurt, and that's what Tox had warned her about, right? "I've already done that once today."

Samantha punched her in the arm. "What? For this?"

"Ow. Why did you do that?"

"Because we just ate dinner and you didn't mention a word about an *emergency*? Are you dying? Do you have lung cancer?"

"Jeez, Sam. No, I just had a little fire at the clinic."

"Little *fire*?" Samantha's voice was almost a shriek. "Are you serious?"

"Just in the air conditioning. I might have inhaled a little smoke. Oh, and maybe I passed out. But only for a second."

Sam grabbed Grace by the arm she was still rubbing from the punching. "March."

"Hey."

"To the fire station."

Grace felt like a mule digging in her heels and pulling backward. "No way."

"It's that or I call 911."

"I don't know what's worse."

"*Walk*."

Samantha had that look in her eye, the one Grace had always recognized as the one she wasn't going to get around. She'd had that look before she bought her first motorcycle. And when she'd insisted on following a drummer across the country to Maine. Luckily, she'd had that look a few weeks into rehab, too. Grace loved that her little sister was as stubborn—no, more—than she was.

It was unfortunate in situations like this, though.

CHAPTER 5

Tox couldn't think of much more he liked better than standing outside with a bowl of ice cream on a warm summer night at the firehouse, watching women go by in workout gear. The guys were inside playing dice for who did the dishes. He was immune, since he'd done them last night.

Three scoops in his bowl, one coffee, one peanut butter, one chocolate. He'd added about four pounds of hot fudge and a metric ton of caramel, just to even the score. Hank had taken one look at it and said, "You're an idiot."

"*You* are." It had been the only appropriate answer, really.

"Where's your whipped cream? Where's the cherry? Where're the nuts?"

Tox said, "This is a snack, not a sundae, and I got all the nuts I need. Wanna see 'em?"

"You don't know anything about dessert," Hank said disgustedly, reaching for the door of the freezer.

Now, outside, his mouth full of ice cream, he watched with appreciation the two women doing a jog-walk down the sidewalk. For some reason, the street the firehouse sat on saw a lot of exercise activity. All the runner-MILFs liked to run down Lowry. Some of them stopped at the bench in front to "stretch." More than one firefighter had nabbed a hose bunny under the flagpole, but Tox had never been desperate like that. He wasn't the type for relationships.

He kind of sucked at them, that was the truth. And he hated doing things he wasn't good at. Okay, sex he was good at, or at least he'd been told that often enough he kind of believed it. He tried his best, that was for sure, and he liked trying. He just wasn't good at the rest of it.

Fine by him. If he had a girlfriend waiting for his call, he wouldn't be able to ogle without guilt, and the two women walking at a fast trot were enough to slow his spoon.

The one in front, who appeared to be dragging the other by the arm was a leggy brunette who looked familiar. She got more so the closer she got. The one behind her—the one with the huge brown eyes wearing a black running skirt—was the woman from earlier. The Rowe sisters, Samantha and Grace.

Now, what were the odds of *that*?

Tox set the bowl of ice cream on the bench. "Ladies," he said.

"She's having a heart attack."

His adrenaline pumped. He'd expected flirting. Not another medical.

"I am not," said Grace. "I just had trouble catching my breath for a second. Now I'm fine."

"Sit," he said. "Here, on the grass."

"I'm totally serious," Grace said. "I'm fine. I don't want or need medical attention. Samantha overreacts." But she sat, folding her compact, well-shaped legs carefully under her. Samantha flopped on the grass next to her.

"You have that inhaler on you?"

Grace shook her head, and her messy ponytail flopped back and forth. "I don't need it. You know Samantha, right? Samantha, this is Tox."

He ignored the reintroduction for a moment and reached in his pocket where he'd already stashed his other inhaler. "Here. Use mine."

Grace pulled in her lips and shook her head again.

"Use it," said Samantha. "Or I'll make bacon and grits every morning for the next week and eat it in front of you."

"Jeez," Grace said, accepting it from him. She lifted the edge of her black tank top and wiped off the mouthpiece.

He folded his arms and looked down at her. Jeez, she was a cute little thing. "Cooties all gone?"

She folded her lips around the inhaler and sucked. Her color looked better within seconds.

"She's careful about germs."

Tox nodded. "Immunocompromised?" She didn't look sick, other than pale, but you never knew.

"No!" gasped Grace, releasing her breath. "It's just healthier to avoid them as much as possible. You never know where …" She passed the inhaler back to him. Their fingertips touched. "… something's been."

"Like I said. Cooties. You know it's actually better for your immune system to deal with germs and battle them off, right?"

She tilted her head. "Some say that, and I can see the worth in that argument. But I work with immunocompromised people all the time, so I try to stay healthy. And I really don't know where your lips have been."

She obviously didn't realize how her sentence would sound until it was out of her mouth, and the look on her face was hilarious: two parts shocked, one part amused. Tox could look at her a while, he realized.

He finally turned to Samantha. "Hey. I wasn't ignoring you, I was just paying attention to the patient. You look great. I'd heard you were back in town."

Samantha bounced to her feet and hugged him. Of course she did. California girls. Back in Boston, where he'd grown up, people didn't just hug willy-nilly. People here, though—he'd been at parties where, after being introduced to a perfect stranger, he'd been squeezed. Who *did* that?

Sam's hug was friendly. She smelled like the same soap he'd smelled on Grace earlier. But on Grace, it had been different. Sweeter, somehow. Deeper. For a second, he kinda wished he was hugging Grace instead.

"You okay now?" he said to Grace. "Do I need to pull out another form for you to sign, refusing medical attention?"

She jerked her chin up, obviously not realizing he was teasing her. "I'll sign it. No problem."

"I'm only—" Tox's attention was yanked away from the startling amber color of her eyes in the dusk light by the man who was barreling toward him full-tilt. "What the—"

"Help!" The man, dressed in a t-shirt and shorts, ran barefoot toward Tox, an infant swaddled in blue cradled against his chest. "My baby! Help me, please, *help*!" When he reached Tox, he thrust out the baby as if he were a hot potato. Reflexively, Tox caught him.

No. Not again.

CHAPTER 6

Grace watched, astonished, as a terrified-looking man practically threw a small baby into Tox's arms.

Tox took one look down at the child and barked at Grace, "Go in the side door and yell, as loud as you can, *Infant code blue.*"

Grace ran as fast as she could. In her haste she couldn't find the side door, so she went through the huge open doors to the big room where the fire engines were housed. It was dark, coming from the outside, but she found an interior door and pulled.

"Infant code blue!" she yelled. She choked and yelled it again. She didn't see anyone. She ran farther into the fire station, down a short hall where matching yellow coats hung on high hooks, and yelled it a third time. She coughed in terror, and wondered if she should just scream the high, thin scream that was threatening the back of her throat. Help. She needed *help.*

She heard boots hit the floor. Two men were at her side, bags in hand. Apparently they were the magic words.

"Where?"

Grace pointed with a shaking finger. "Front. Outside."

She stayed at their heels. The one who had been with Tox earlier, the man he'd called Coin yelled over his shoulder, "Is it your baby? Girl or boy? Age?"

"Not mine," she gasped.

Outside, Tox had dropped to his knees on the grass. The father hovered over him, and Samantha was standing a few feet away, her hand over her mouth.

"Sir, I need you to back up a few steps so we can work, okay? How old is your son?"

"Three months. But he was a preemie. My wife called 911, but I thought it would be faster to run here ..."

Tox laid the blanket the baby was wrapped in on the grass. The child was rigid, his eyes open and glassy, his jaw gritted, his fingers flexed.

Grace was pretty sure he wasn't breathing.

"For the love of Pete," spat Tox. "What if we'd been out on a call?" He did something with the baby's neck as Coin inserted a plastic mouthpiece into a clear bag. "Has he been feverish?"

The father looked as if he were watching his worst nightmare come true in front of his eyes. "Yeah. We've been giving him baby acetaminophen—did that cause it?"

Tox shook his head as he tilted the baby's chin. "No." But he didn't reassure the man, either. He just spoke quickly, words that Grace didn't understand, instructing what each firefighter should do. "Febrile seizure. Postictal. Compressions if he doesn't breathe in about twenty seconds."

The other two firefighters nodded, their hands full, poised to act on Tox's command.

Grace watched, holding her breath in her chest. Tox's hands were so big, so wide, and yet his touch on the tiny boy were small and precise. It was almost delicate, the way he lowered his head to put his ear next to the baby's mouth. No cars passed. Even the birds were silent, as if everyone was waiting.

"He's got air," said Tox. His voice was professional, unshaken. The baby gave a strange, small gasp, and then grabbed another one. Color flooded back into his face—he went mottled blue and red, and then turned an unholy plum color.

Coin said to the father, "He'll be fine."

Grace forgot to look at the father's face—she was too busy staring at Tox's.

There was no one else in his world at that moment. She had the feeling that if a car exploded or a meteor crashed behind them right now, the other firefighters would scramble to do what had to be done, but Tox—he wouldn't move. He wouldn't stop what he was doing— hooking up what looked like oxygen to the baby's nose with the smallest piece of plastic. Who made that plastic? Who could possibly be responsible for manufacturing plastic for inserting into tiny children's noses like that? Tox looked enormous, hunched over the child, but his huge fingers looked unbelievably gentle touching the baby's nose. Earlier, when she'd seen him at her clinic, he'd moved as if he were caged, constantly rocking on his heels, pushing his fist into his palm, as if energy was roiling under his skin. Now, he was still. Contained. Almost ... peaceful looking.

An ambulance had pulled out of the garage and already had the back doors standing open. A female firefighter said, "Sir? Do you want to come with us in the back?"

The man nodded numbly.

Tox appeared reluctant to hand the child to the woman.

A pretty woman with a short blond bob, she smiled at him encouragingly. "Come on, Tox."

Tox handed over the baby and turned to the father. "Name?"

The father jumped and touched his chest. "Me? John Murray."

Tox shook his head impatiently. "Baby."

"Johnny. His name is Johnny."

A smile crossed Tox's face, and Grace noticed small lines at the corners of his eyes. "Great name. Strong little guy you have there."

Relief wreathed the man's expression. He launched himself at Tox in a hug. Grace watched as Tox went completely rigid, but he managed to give the man a light pat on the back. Then the man leaped into the ambulance. Tox turned his back on them, gathering gear off the lawn. A firefighter Grace hadn't seen before said something about the Angel of Death being vanquished. Tox's mouth twisted, but then he gave what sounded like a grudging laugh, his relief audible.

Samantha tapped Grace on the elbow. "We should probably go," she whispered.

Grace jumped. "What? Yeah."

Samantha was all eyes. She looked pale. She'd never done that well around medical problems. When their mother was sick, Sam had been great at dealing with doctors, leaving Grace to take physical care of their mother. It had been a good, fair division of labor. Now Grace put her arm around Samantha's shoulders.

"You ready to finish our walk?"

Sam's eyes got bigger. "Really? We have to do that?"

Tox turned to face them. He'd gone back to looking like he had caffeine in his blood. His posture was rigid. Ready.

"Just walk down to the breakwater and get a cinnamon roll at Josie's Bakery Or a sundae at Skip's."

Sam grabbed Grace's hand. "Skip's Peanutter Blast."

Grace shook her head. "No way. We're out here being healthy."

"Screw that," said Tox. "You see that baby?" He pointed at the ambulance pulling on to the street. "You never know in life. You might get hit by a car on the walk home."

"Cheery thought."

"Have ice cream first." He looked down at his hands, hands that had just been cradling a tiny life. "You won't regret it."

It was surprisingly sweet, coming from the man who seemed to have no soft edges. Grace felt herself melting like the ice cream still in the bowl Tox had put on the bench.

"Yeah," she said. "Come on, Sam. Peanutter Blast it is."

As they walked away, Grace could almost feel his gaze on her back. She tuned out Samantha's chatter for a moment and steeled herself to look behind her. To meet those sea-green eyes. To see if doing so would make her heart skip again in that strange rhythm she didn't really enjoy.

She pulled her head high and pretended to look up in the sky, as if a plane were flying low overhead. Then she turned to look at him.

He was gone.

CHAPTER 7

The next day in dispatch, Lexie gave Tox a rash of abuse. After ten minutes of good-natured ribbing, Tox said, "Come on. It's not like I was gonna adopt the kid."

"Really? Because I heard you were about to pull up your shirt and let little Johnny look for milk."

Tox sighed and popped the chair so that it reclined backward. "I was just doing my job. You know, my very *important* job. Unlike you, I get to actually get off my ass and save lives every once in a while."

Lexie threw a pencil at him. He caught it left-handed and threw it back at her. She missed. She always did.

"Oh, yeah?" she said. "That guy on Route 119 that coded last week? You saw what his wife was like. And who talked her down? Got her to listen? Told her how to do CPR that guaranteed she wasn't gonna get his life insurance quite yet?" She stuck two thumbs into her chest. "That would be *moi.*"

Tox rubbed his neck. "Yeah, whatever. Field save, phone save, he's still got to go sometime. We just put it off for a little while. Probably not for long. That man looked like he buttered his bacon."

"Is that sexual?" Lexie raised a cheerful eyebrow. "Because I'm so ready to sue someone."

"Good luck with that."

Lexie was a good dispatcher, and over the years, Tox had learned what that meant in terms of his job. A good dispatcher could mean the difference between a good tour and a bad tour. A bad dispatcher could mean the difference between life and death, literally. Lexie was his favorite dispatcher, and he considered her a friend. Maybe she didn't know that, exactly. It wasn't like he advertised how he felt about people by taking out skywriters. But she listened to his whining. She laughed at him, and she didn't put up with his bull. During some shifts, he wouldn't even walk down the hall to dispatch. But when Lexie was working, he routinely spent an hour or more shooting the crap with her. She was smart and funny, and knew how to multitask like it was no one's business. He'd been in dispatch and watched her give baby-birthing instructions while jotting directions to the county fair and eating a bowl of chili at the same time. "This job's easy," she always said. "As long as you're a schizophrenic octopus."

Now she answered a non-emergency line and said with a sweet-as-honey voice, "Sorry, that's through fire prevention, sir, and they're closed on the weekend. Can you call on Monday? They can help you find a weed abatement company then." She hung up with a click on her numeric pad and said, "Idiots. Can't even go to Dan's Hardware and buy their own flipping weed whacker." She looked at Tox. "How *hard* is that? People! What are we, babysitters?"

Another thing Tox liked about Lexie was her attitude. That and her tattoos, green vines with black roses that trailed out of both short sleeves of her uniform polo shirt. "Yup."

"I need a raise," she said.

Tox rubbed his neck. Blast it, it ached. Something about being bent over that kid had tweaked it again—it had been hurting something fierce ever since last night.

"What's wrong with you?" demanded Lexie.

"Nothin'. Where are those Red Vines you had last tour?"

"I ate 'em. Is that your neck thing acting up again?"

"No."

"Liar," Lexie said, stabbing the pen in his direction. "That's the injury you got last year in that garage fire."

"No way." Tox had never gone after worker's comp—way too much paperwork, and he had been scared of the time they might make him take off. Lexie was one of the few people in the department he'd told about it.

"You're so bad at lying. Your eyes go all squinty and creepy."

"Creepy?" He'd take a lot from her, but not that. "My eyes don't get creepy."

"Like you're outside my window peeping in."

"Dream on, woman. I'm not into redheads."

"Seriously, how many times do I have to lecture you about this?"

"I can give you a good answer for that. None."

She held her right hand up, palm out. "I took an oath."

"Oh, please."

"Serve and protect. I serve the citizens and protect you guys."

He scoffed, "You give us heartburn with your addiction to red chili pepper, that's what you give us."

"My friend's an acupuncturist. You have to go see her."

Instead of rolling his eyes, as he would have any other day of the year, Tox felt the skin prickle on the back of his neck. He tried to play it cool, like he had no idea what acupuncture even was. "Nah."

"Hey! That's where the air conditioner fire was yesterday. At Grace's clinic? That was One's zone, right?" She tapped a few keys and peered at one of the five screens in front of her. "Yeah. I knew it. You went there yesterday. Was my friend Grace Rowe there?"

He shrugged and looked up at the ceiling.

"Squinty! Creepy!"

"Yeah, I met her. The quack, right?"

"It's not quackery. I swear to you. You know how I know?"

Tox sighed. "How?"

"My brother's cat."

"Oh, come on."

"Mr. Sniffles. He got hit by a car, and his ass got broken so that he peed all over the house."

"That sounds amazing."

Lexie hit a button on the side of her chair. It sunk down so she could sit back and stick her legs out straight. "Yeah, it was great. The house smelled like a litter box, only a little worse. They had to manually pee him. I didn't even know you could do that to a cat. Twice a day, they hoisted him up onto a pile of paper towels and squeezed his bladder till he peed."

"No freaking way. I have to deal with enough catheters in my line of work."

"Yeah. So, his wife wanted Mr. Sniffles put down. I have to say, I can see the argument there. I didn't know what kind of a life it was for Mr. Sniffles to drag himself around the house like that. He didn't even look comfortable.

But James was desperate to save his cat. Went everywhere, talked to everyone. Someone suggested acupuncture at some place up in Eureka. It was a day off for me, and there's a sushi place we like there, so I went along for the ride, thinking I'd get a good laugh and some great baked scallop nigiri."

"Everything about this conversation is gross."

"I didn't believe in it at all. The acupuncturist, though, he kind of just looked like anyone else in Eureka. Jeans, carefully groomed facial hair. More hipster than hippie, you know? And Mr. Sniffles is *freaking* because it smells like a vet's office, and he's been in about a million of them. James puts the cat on the table and holds him down. He's getting scratched, and Mr. Sniffles is fighting, and the doctor doesn't even trip. He just sticks a couple of these little needles into the cat. And then the craziest thing happened."

Tox couldn't help asking, "What?"

"Mr. Sniffles started to purr."

"Huh."

"No, dude, that's big. He started to purr and then he conked out, fast asleep like the doctor had drugged him or something. James is standing there openmouthed, and the doctor just walks out, saying he would leave them in for about twenty minutes."

"So did the cat get up and walk?"

The radio blared.

"Ladder Three, Darling copies, in quarters." Lexie let off the foot pedal and typed for a second. Then she turned back to him. "Nah. He was just the same."

"What the point of this story? That acupuncture makes cats purr?"

"It means cats don't know what the needles are supposed to do to them. But they react to it, without knowing. And yeah, after about twelve sessions, that dang cat was peeing on his own again, jumping in and out of the litter box. It was crazy."

Tox said, "He probably just finally healed."

"Sure. That was obvious. But something made him finally heal, and the only thing that changed was the acupuncture. And for me, it helps my insomnia."

Tox pulled at the edge of a sticker on the side of the phone monitor.

"Stop that." She slapped his hand. "I'm going to give you two sessions with her."

He would have to spend more time with Grace if Lexie did that. No, he didn't think so. Tox didn't want that.

Except that he did. "Nah," he made himself say.

Lexie swung in her chair to yet another computer. "I'm doing it." She punched the keyboard, minimizing the page she'd been on and bringing up another one.

"Wait, what was that?" He recognized the web page she'd tried to hide. He'd been on it once, with crappy results.

"Nothing."

"That was HoldMe.com, right?"

"No." Lexie scowled.

"It was. Don't lie to me, Lex. Are you on the prowl?"

Lexie stopped typing and lifted her eyes to his. She had red wavy hair that she piled up out of her way with one of those plastic clips with all the teeth. Her headset was usually crooked, though she straightened it every time the phone rang. She was pleasantly rounded, curved in all the right places, and the tattoos she sported gave her a little edge. Other guys in the station considered her hot, but Tox had always seen her as more of a little sister than anything, someone to tease mercilessly.

"No!" she said again.

"Why were you looking at that site, then?"

She narrowed her eyes. "You're way too nosy. I hate it when you get like this."

"Like what?"

"Like you have the right to know what I do when I'm here. You don't."

Tox felt a pinprick of something that hurt a little, though he didn't want to admit it. "I thought I was your friend."

"Oh, shut up," she said, but her face softened.

"Really," he said. "I don't *need* to know what you do when you're not here—"

"Which, with all my overtime, is basically never," she pointed out.

"True. But it does matter to me that you're happy. And that if you date, that it's a nice guy." Tox said, grabbing her blue squishy stress ball off her desk and smashing it, ignoring the strain he felt in his neck.

"Dang, Ellis." She only used his last name when she was surprised. "That's kind of a sweet thing to say. Are you feeling okay?"

"Just don't go on any dates with serial killers, okay?"

"If I do," she said, pulling her wallet out of her purse, "I'll be sure to let you know before we go out so you can track him down later."

He pointed to her credit card. "What are you doing?"

"Gift certificate." Lexie entered her card numbers faster than he ever could have. When Tox used the computer in the day room to type up his reports, he had to hunt and peck with two fingers, and it always hurt his neck. Which was why Susie Costello at Admin was always breathing down his neck about missing reports.

"No, don't—"

"Too late." She tapped something loudly and the printer began to spit out a piece of paper. "You are no match for technology." She held it out to him. "Take it."

"No."

"Fine." She put it on her desk and started folding it.

Tox watched.

Sixty seconds later, Lexie sailed a perfect paper airplane at his head. It hit him square in the middle of the forehead. "Now take it. And go. If you don't get fixed, you're gonna end up on light duty, in here with me, and neither of us would be able to stand that."

Muttering under his breath, he folded it and shoved it in his back pocket. "You're not a very nice person," he said as he left the room.

"Screw you, too." She flipped him off and followed it with a blown kiss.

"Thanks, Lexie."

911 rang. "You're welcome." *Tap.* "911, what's the address of the emergency?"

CHAPTER 8

Grace was getting used to the rhythm of the clinic, settling in. Finally. It felt good. The first year she'd been open, she hadn't known what to expect. She could go from busy to dead in the space of fifteen minutes. About six months ago, she'd had a Friday on which every scheduled patient had canceled and she'd gotten no walk-ins, not one. It had scared her so badly she'd spent her whole weekend on the computer, setting up advertising, brainstorming ways to get the clinic's name out there. And then, that following Monday, she'd been so busy she'd never gotten a chance to eat lunch. She hadn't even had her tea.

This Monday morning she had three appointments scheduled, and she hoped for more walk-ins. But usually no one came in before ten except for Mrs. Finch who got up at five every morning because she said a day without a sunrise was a day wasted. Grace tended to think that was a little overboard. The sun came up without her worrying about it. Most days, anyway.

She walked out onto the front porch of her practice. She'd managed to grab the little Victorian cottage when it had come on the market, when it was still a fixer-upper. She'd put her own sweat equity into it, taking months to get everything done before opening. It had been a mark of pride, though, learning how to redo drywall (the previous owners had a son who liked to put his fist through the wall when he was angry, which seemed to have been way too often) and how to retile the roof. The fact that she knew how the bathroom was plumbed made her confident she'd know what to do if the sink started leaking again. It felt more like home here, at the practice, than her own small house did, a quarter mile away.

Grace set her mug of tea on the porch rail and looked out onto Iris Street. From here, if she stood on tiptoe, she could look over Felicia Dow's low gabled roof and catch just a glimpse of Darling Bay. On foggy summer mornings like this, sound was captured and carried farther than normal. The noise of the seals barking down by the fishing pier lifted her spirits. She hugged her old blue sweater tightly around her and felt thankful, again, that she'd chosen the right town. She'd been raised inland, in a hot, dusty, farming community. Her father had grown strawberries, and while they'd hired pickers every season, she and her sister Samantha had been on the permanent staff, even being kept out of class during the height of the season. It had been worth it, to her father, to have the extra four hands working, even when he had to deal with the phone calls from school. "They're my kids, and if I say they're sick, they're sick, and you have no right to come and check on them." He would bang the phone down and point. "Pick as fast as you can, and we'll get McD's tonight." To Grace and Samantha, to whom McDonald's was the height of elegance and refinement, this was payment enough.

Their father had stayed in the field until he died of skin

cancer while Grace was in college. Their mother had died of a rare lung disease two years later. They were all sure it came from inhaling years of crop dust, but who could they appeal to? No one. Grace had tried so hard, to fix them both, to get them out, to get them healed, and nothing had worked.

Escaping to the cool, foggy beach town of Darling Bay was the best thing she could have done. In the ten years she'd been here, Samantha had been with her, on and off, a year here and a year there. Grace cherished the time with her sister, trying not to grasp her too tightly, like she knew she sometimes did. She had to let her sister breathe. Knowing that and letting her sister have her own life, though, were two different things.

A motorcycle took the corner at Taylor and First Street a little too fast. Speed demons always liked coming down First for its tight curve along the marina, but Grace hated it when they raced past her practice. The noise was one thing—the roar and gas fumes that came out of their tailpipes—but her real concern was safety. Someday she'd have to run out there to scoop one up off the roadway. She'd be the first person on scene, and yes, while she was CPR trained, she sure as heck never wanted to have to use it. Lifesaving was for people like Tox.

Big, strong, grumpy Tox. The man wouldn't leave her thoughts.

The motorcycle paused, slowed, and then stopped in front. Great. Would he leave it parked there? In her best customer parking spot?

The man got off the bike in one smooth motion, making it look like it weighed nothing beneath him.

Then, as if she'd conjured him merely by thinking his name, the man took off his helmet.

Tox.

He looked criminally sexy. In his black leather jacket, he looked more like he was about to knock over a liquor store with a sawed-off shotgun rather than stride confidently up the three steps to her porch.

One thing she knew—he *was* a robber, because she couldn't quite get back the breath she kept losing when he was around.

"Hey," he said. The helmet hung lightly from a finger against his thigh. His wide, jean-clad thigh.

"You actually like riding that thing?"

"It's nice to see you, too."

Grace realized she hadn't responded to his opening salvo very appropriately, but she didn't care that much. "You know the risks of riding a motorcycle?"

"Not off the top of my head, no." He took off his black leather jacket and laid it down on her porch swing. As if he owned the place.

"You're thirty-five times more likely to die in a crash than a person in a car, did you know that? And forty-eight percent of motorcycle crashes are a direct result of speeding."

"I did know that, actually. I don't speed unless I'm alone on the highway." He dragged his hand through his dark blond hair. Shaggy, and with just the right amount of curl to it, it looked amazing when he stopped. Grace knew that if she'd ever put a helmet on, she'd end up with worse hair than she did when she wore a baseball cap. But this guy looked tousled. She bet he always looked that good. *Boy,* that was annoying.

So she continued, "A little less than half of all motorcycle deaths involve only the motorcyclist."

Tox almost smiled—she could tell he did. "How do you know all this?"

*Years of worrying about Samantha and her stupid motorcycle which she finally sold for drug money before she got clean the last time.*

"I know stuff."

"How are you feeling?"

Oh. Tox was checking up on her. "You probably want your inhaler back. Hang on, it's inside."

He raised a hand. "I'm fine. I have more of them. Keep it."

"You didn't have to come here," she said. It came out more gracelessly than she would have liked. "I mean, thank you so much. The way you helped me on Friday—twice—was great. I can't tell you how much I appreciate it. But I'm happy to take care of myself, and I know what to do for difficulty breathing."

"You're going to stick needles in yourself?" Tox looked horrified.

"With that," she said, "and the right herbs, I'll be right as rain in no time."

"Oh. Well," he said, and ran his hand through his hair again.

Grace wished he would stop doing that. It was distracting.

"Anyway," she said pointedly. "Thanks."

"It was nice to see your sister."

Ah, that was the game, then. It had been a long time since Grace had needed to fend off guys at the front door, but she remembered it well. "It's good to have her back in town."

"Must be."

Grace waited, cupping her tea in her hands. He would

follow up with a request for Sam's phone number or at the very least a query about her relationship status.

"Coffee's a good thing to have," he said, gesturing. Was he uncomfortable? Why was he shifting from one foot to the other like that?

"I drink tea."

"Huh. Why?"

"Lower cortisol response." That was the truth of it, but actually, she still had a cup of coffee or two in the mornings. She hadn't been able to cut herself off  yet.

"Okay ..."

Grace finally took pity on him. "Can I help you with something? Do you need to check the air conditioner? Because a friend of mine is in HVAC and he came in on Saturday. I got a whole new unit. It's quieter than the last unit, but I can show you if you need me to."

"I was actually..."

She waited again. Whatever he wanted to say, it was something he didn't really like. She could read it in the way he held his eyes, tight and careful, and the way his mouth was folded, as if he'd tasted something sour. And heck. Even with his mouth pressed that way, he still had a sexy mouth. Fine, strong lips.

Grace jerked herself back to the present. She nodded in what she hoped was an encouraging way. "So ..."

"Can you stick some of those needles in me?"

"Pardon?" She must not have heard him right.

He looked even more pained. "I got a gift certificate. I'm supposed to ..."

"Oh! Lexie! I saw that come through online."

Tox nodded. "One time she made me do a sweat lodge with her. All I got was a headache from the smoke. She gets me into the most stupid crap."

"Wow," said Grace.

His eyes widening, he hurried to say, "No, I don't mean ... That's not what ..."

Grace laughed. "It's not the first time I've dealt with a skeptic. And I'm sure it won't be the last. Come on in. I've got some paperwork I need you to fill out."

CHAPTER 9

Tox sat in a comfortable and probably ergonomically correct red foam chair in the outer office. It was a pretty room, done up in red and yellow and lots of green. There must have been twenty plants in the small front room alone, their vines twisting around each other. Small purple blooms warred with clusters of white. How did someone get flowers to grow inside like that?

Grace hadn't been kidding about the paperwork. Tox was used to forms—used to dealing with and tracking the paperwork he encountered daily at work—but this was something else. Did she really need to know his sleep pattern (bad) or how many times a week he had sugar (at least seven, if he had ice cream every day, and sometimes he actually had it twice, and was he supposed to admit that too)? She wanted to know about any history of depression (he called it the blues, himself, and given long enough, it usually dissipated like drift smoke). Relationship troubles? That was one place he was good, he knew that. No relationship trouble at all. If you kept yourself happily single, you didn't have any worries in that area.

And he was *not* going to tell her about his bathroom habits. No way.

But the other stuff surprised him. He didn't lie about smoking, because he didn't have to. He'd always hated the habit, and being in his line of work had made him hate it more. How many thousands of breathing calls had he been on over the years? Lung cancer was ugly, uglier than most other ways to die, and he'd seen a lot of it. Nothing fun about drowning to death.

Drinking? Sure, he had a few on the weekends. Lately he might have been having one too many on occasion, and it bothered him to admit it, starkly like that, in blue pen on white paper. It was actually a good reminder for him. It didn't take very many to be too many. He resolved, sitting there, that he was going to let his bottle of Scotch maybe pick up a few cobwebs. He didn't need it, and he didn't ever want to.

Grace had given him a cup of tea in a green and white ceramic mug when he'd sat down with the questionnaire, and he took a sip absently.

Okay, normally tea wasn't his thing, not even when they gave it to you free at Su's Chinese on Fourth. This was different, though. It wasn't sweet, but there was something to it ... vanilla? Something sweet. Kind of the same scent he'd smelled on her last week, actually.

"You ready?" she said, reentering the small room.

He nodded. "Hey, you sure you have time for me today? Because I can come back another time."

"This way," she said, leading him into the next room. He hadn't even given the room a second glance when he was there for the air conditioner fire on Friday, but now he took his time looking around. In another lifetime, this room was probably the parlor of the old Victorian. It was narrow, but it ran long. Green plants in brightly painted pots were everywhere, giving the room a lush, verdant feel. The walls were covered with red velvet wallpaper, the design ornate. While it should have made the room seem heavy and dark, the many windows, most of them standing open, made the room feel airy. The place where her fire extinguisher should have hung was still empty.

He pointed. "You need to buy another one."

"I have it in my car."

"No good to you out there." Tox turned slowly. He counted ten simple recliners, nothing like the plush, heavy ones they had at work.

"You can fill all these chairs with patients? At the same time?"

"Sometimes," she said easily. "I have a couple of private rooms for people who don't want to share. Would you prefer that?"

And have her think he was shy? No way.

"That's okay. I know I didn't have an appointment and all. I guess I should have called." He jerked his head in the direction of the way they'd come. "You want me to come back another day?"

She gestured to the empty recliners. "Shoes off, please."

"Oh." He'd been halfway hoping he'd get out of it. Maybe she'd even tell Lexie he'd come by, and then she'd get off his back.

"I actually have a pretty full afternoon. It's good that you've come now. A patient's first appointment is the most important, and it's the one that takes the longest."

What was she planning to *do* to him?

"As you saw," Grace said while pointing him to the recliner nearest the stereo, "this is my main treatment room."

Was he supposed to just sit down? She wasn't going to take his blood pressure or his weight or anything? He tugged at the laces on his work boots, all he really ever wore anymore. At least he didn't have feet like Chief Barger—that smell could kill a possum half a mile away.

"Right there's perfect." She pulled out a rolling stool from under a counter and placed it next to his recliner. "Go ahead and tilt it back," she said, now standing at the shelves on the north wall. "I want you to make yourself as comfortable as possible."

"Because this is going to hurt, huh?"

She took a folded white towel and a peach-colored blanket from a shelf. "Are you scared of needles?"

"No." Tox felt a thin sheen of sweat break at his hairline.

"Really?" She was close to him again, that same sweet-tea vanilla smell in his nose. Man, he liked that smell. He inhaled and felt something inside of himself ease.

"I don't think I am," said Tox.

"But you're nervous."

He shrugged and sent the recliner backward. Yeah, there was the same sweet spot as the ones at the station. Get the feet adjusted right, and the head in that comfortable zone, and you could just bliss out, no matter what dumb crap your partner was watching on the big screen TV. "Not nervous. Maybe just a little ... concerned."

"Here," she said, leaning over him, draping the blanket over his legs. "Adjust this so that you're warm enough."

"Are you kidding me?"

"Too warm?"

"I'm sweating here."

She removed the blanket and draped it over the next chair. "Are you *sure* you're not scared of needles?"

"They're sterilized, right?"

Grace laughed, a light, pretty sound. "Of course. Each one has never been used." She glanced down at her paperwork. "Why do they call you Tox?"

The change of subject startled him. "What?"

"Is it short for Toxic?"

"Yeah."

"Why?"

"I'm a hazardous materials guy." He paused. "Kind of *the* hazmat guy. If something bad blows up or off-gasses, they want me around to analyze it."

She looked down at his paperwork. "What's your real name?"

"Nuh-uh. If you need that for insurance or the gift certificate or something, I'll just pay cash."

"No, no, I'm just curious, that's all."

Tox cleared his throat. "How many needles are you planning on using?"

"Not that many. A hundred and thirty or so?"

He jerked upright. "No way. No freakin' way. Screw Lexie and her bright ideas."

She laughed again and put a cool hand on his forearm. "I'm teasing you. We'll probably do between ten and twenty points today. But at any time, if you feel uncomfortable, or if you want to leave, you can."

He tried to relax back into the chair, but it was hard. The fight-or-flight reflex left the webs between his fingers damp. He hoped he wasn't sweating through his shirt. "What's the towel for?"

Sitting on the stool and rolling closer to him, holding his paperwork, she said, "I would tell you it's to mop up your blood, but I think I'm at the edge of too much teasing with you."

Tox pushed out his chest. "Impossible."

"Really?" She stuck the tip of her pen lightly into his forearm, and Tox jumped so high he felt his neck protest in response. "Ow," he said. "Man."

"I'm sorry," Grace said, leaning forward again. "I don't usually do that."

"Scare people into tweaking their necks?"

"Tease patients."

Tox had to admit, he liked it in theory. He liked being teased, especially by a woman so hot he could barely look away from her. Yeah, his neck hurt, but the trade-off was that he got to stare at those big coffee-colored eyes of hers.

Not a bad trade, really.

CHAPTER 10

Grace felt like an idiot. A terribly *young* idiot, who wouldn't have passed her California licensing exam if she'd done anything like that. Teasing a patient until she hurt him! What had she been thinking?

She wasn't. That was the point. Around Tox, she acted like a twelve-year-old girl, too young to understand why she wanted to poke a boy in the shoulder as she ran past him in dodge ball.

Taking a deep breath, she grounded herself for a moment, placing her feet flat on the floor.

Grace was a helper. She would help Tox. It was what he needed. The fact that he made her hormones swirl like he'd stuck a spoon in them and stirred, that wasn't his fault. She was the pro here.

"Okay. This is to prop yourself on if you want it. It looks like your neck hurts." Rolling the towel, she kept her gaze firmly on the area his fingers were absentmindedly rubbing. She carefully didn't meet his eyes, worried that if she did, she'd want to tickle him next, or worse. "It might help to have this behind it."

He leaned forward so that she could tuck the towel behind his head.

"I'm going to check your pulses now."

As she reached forward to hold his wrist, she felt Tox watching her closely.

She straightened her back and concentrated on feeling the blood and energy move under her fingertips. He felt strong. Vital.

"Okay." She rolled so that she was at his feet. "I'm going to roll up the bottoms of your jeans now." With some people, Grace was careful to talk them through every step of the process. He was one of those people who needed it, and she was having a hard time forgiving herself for being so unaware that she might have scared him.

It was just hard to believe that a man who looked like he did could be scared of anything.

"Now I'll take the pulses at your feet."

Tox snorted. Grace looked up sharply.

"Sorry," he said. "Sorry. Keep going."

Grace palpated his foot gently.

"Will I live?"

She patted him—a professional touch, sure—on the ankle and moved around, rolling up to his other wrist. "Probably."

Wrapping her fingers around his right wrist, she listened. She'd had a lot of education, yes. She'd trained for years in not only Eastern but Western medicine, too. She'd be paying her student loans back for the rest of her life. But this—listening to the body with her hands—was more than just learning where to place your fingers. She unfocused her eyes and let herself hear what the blood was saying in this man's thick wrist.

She'd expected thready. She could tell Tox wasn't in the

habit of taking care of himself. But instead, she felt his energy moving quickly. It was wide and full. It was what one of her teachers would have called "a rebellious Qi." Its rhythm was hurried—that didn't surprise her. She liked the way his pulse felt under her fingertips. And that fact—the unprofessionalism of it—unnerved her more than his strength.

A grip. She had to get one. "May I see your tongue, please?"

A lazy smile spread across his face. "I didn't think this was that kind of place, but sure, babe."

He was *trying* to rattle her.

But she wouldn't be rattled. Nope. "Thanks. Just stick it out for me."

So close. She was so close to him.

"Okay." She cleared her throat. "Have you ever had trouble with your gallbladder?"

He shook his head.

He smelled of soap, a green scent, and lightly, of sweat. But his breath was sweet. "You can put your tongue away now, thanks."

"There are so many responses I want to make to that ..." he said.

"Well, you don't have to." Grace rolled her stool backward and grabbed the needle box from the low Chinese table. "I've probably heard them all. Tell me about your body." As soon as the words left her mouth, she wanted to take them back.

A low laugh. "I think we're moving a little too fast, sugar. Don't I get to buy you dinner first?"

She prayed her cheeks weren't flushing the way she felt they might be. "Tell me about your back issues."

His eyes narrowed. "My back is fine."

"Really?" His posture was protective, even now, sitting in the most relaxed position possible. His elbows were tight at his sides, his legs pushing tension toward her so that she could feel it in waves.

But she kept her voice light as she gestured to her own neck. "You seem to be rubbing right here."

With a guilty expression, he dropped his hand. "Just a little tight. In the neck. Not my back."

Grace nodded. "Sometimes the neck is the way the back gets our attention." She picked up a needle. "We have a place to address that, don't worry."

"*Ooof.*" He winced.

"I haven't touched you yet." Why did everything she said come out sounding dirty? Grace had never had this problem before. When she'd been getting her Master's, one of her fellow students had fallen in love with a patient who frequented the student clinic. It had been the scandal of the year, and she'd never completed her training. Grace remember thinking, *You shouldn't be in the job if you can't keep your hands to yourself when it matters.*

And right now, all she could think about was the way his skin felt under her fingertips, rough and hard and somehow ... sweet, too. Dang it all. She had to get a grip.

"Okay, have a look at this." She rolled back toward him, conscious of going slowly. "See how tiny it is? Thinner than a human hair."

"It's still a needle."

"But look, it's so flexible."

"You can't pierce skin with a human hair. Therefore, that's a needle."

Grace warmed up. This was the part she was best at. "Just lie back. You can keep your eyes open or close them, whatever's most comfortable to you. I'll press on different areas of your skin and ask you questions, and then I'll put in the points. If it's an area where you need work, it will zing."

"You mean hurt."

"I mean twinge. Just a little." She touched the skin between his thumb and first finger lightly. "I'll put the first one here."

Tox sat back with his eyes closed. Then he opened them again. Yep, she knew he'd be a watcher. He wasn't the kind of man who liked to relinquish control over anything at all. "Do it," he said.

"I already did."

"Huh?" Yanking his hand toward his face, he examined the needle wobbling in the back of his hand. "Ow."

"Really? Does that actually hurt?"

"No," he said slowly. "So freaking weird. I didn't feel you put it in."

"Don't worry," said Grace. "You will."

# CHAPTER 11

She was right. Tox felt three of the needles stab him like tiny little vicious knives. She put one a few inches above his ankle, and he almost came right off the chair. "What are you *doing?*"

"Mmm," she said. "Have you been craving sugar lately?"

All the time. Every day. Morning and night. "Nah, not that much."

"Huh, that surprises me."

The pain, as sharp as it was, was precise and lasted only a second. Most of the needles he didn't feel at all, not even as a tickle.

"That's bizarre," Tox said, marveling at the way the needles danced and bobbed in his arms as if they were dancing on air currents. Maybe they were.

"Now just relax," Grace said, snapping the box shut. She swiveled to face him. "Are you comfortable? Warm enough?"

She was so dang pretty. That was the thing. The more Tox looked at her, the more he *liked* looking at her. Her skin was practically radiant. Shoot. That's not the way he needed to think. Next thing he knew he'd be spouting poetry about flowers and kittens at her. And her lashes were so long he thought they might tangle if she slept on her pillow the wrong way. "Are you wearing that ... black stuff?"

Tox knew the word he was looking for, but his brain was suddenly too relaxed to work very hard to come up with it.

"Excuse me?" She blinked hard, and her maple-syrup eyes seemed even prettier.

He blinked back. "You know. That stuff that makes your lashes long."

Grace bit her lower lip and a fingertip brushed her eye. "Mascara? No. I forgot to put any on this morning. I didn't think anyone ..."

She didn't think what? That anyone would be looking at her eyes? How could people not? Tox felt something warm in his abdomen and let his own eyes droop for a moment.

"Just rest," she said in a soft voice. "I might have other drop-ins, but try your best to ignore what else might be going on in the room. I'll keep my eye on you and when you're ready, just let me know."

That woke Tox up a little. "How will I know when I'm ready?"

She smiled, and he noticed for the first time that when she did, a dimple dug deeply into her right cheek. It made her a little bit lopsided and even cuter. Well, shoot.

Tox was nursing a full-on crush.

It had been a long time since he'd felt this. It was kind of fun. He let his eyes drift closed again. This morning if anyone had told him he would have fallen asleep in public, he would have called that person stark-plumb crazy, maybe worse. It just felt good sitting here, that was all. Sitting in the room full of plants, a ray of sun slanting over his knees.

He could hear Grace rustling around in another room, and he pictured her, tucking an errant strand of hair behind her ear. The phone rang softly, and he heard her voice talking low enough that he couldn't make out the words. Somewhere, a clock ticked.

Tox drifted away.

---

"HOW ARE YOU DOING?"

Tox opened his eyes, surprised but not startled to see Grace sitting next to him. Her lips were shiny and pink now. "Sorry. I guess I fell asleep."

"For two hours, yeah."

"No way." At home, he never went more than forty-five minutes without rolling over and looking at his clock. At work, it was even shorter. On nights when they didn't get calls, he still slept with one ear open, waiting for the tones that would convey a structure fire or a medical emergency.

"People don't usually knock out that way for more than thirty minutes, but sometimes I get someone like you. I thought I'd check, though. I didn't know if you had some place to be at a certain time."

"Nah."

Nowhere but here.

"Okay, I'll take out your points."

Tox winced, but he felt them leaving his skin even less than he'd felt them going in.

"How do you feel?" Grace's touch was cool. Professional.

Yeah. His reaction to her was anything but. "Fine," he said.

"Fine is good," she said, wiping at a dot of blood on his wrist he couldn't even feel.

"Maybe ..."

She smiled without meeting his gaze. "Maybe a little better than fine?"

Tox shook his head, forgetting that she hadn't taken out a needle in his ear. His blasted *ear*. "I just don't get how it works."

She sat back, dropping the used needles into a sharps box. "I can tell you all about it if you want me to, but something tells me you're not going to buy what I say about channels of energy."

She was right. He probably wouldn't. But there was that whole story ... "Lexie told me something about a cat."

"Oh, yeah! That's how I met her! She came in here after her brother's cat was helped. That's a great story. And I have to say, you react the same way the cat did."

"Awesome." That was the way he wanted this woman to think of him. Like a danged kitty cat. Nope, he was all tiger. And those little needles made him want to growl with happiness. He wanted to stretch and roll over in his bed, taking her with him.

Where had *that* thought come from? But now, the more he tried not to think it, the more he couldn't help himself. What would that mouth feel like on his? Those shiny lips made him want to taste them, to see if the gloss tasted sweet or if that was just her. Right now, as she leaned over him, checking the point on his forehead where he'd had a needle, he could just put his hand up, behind her neck ...

And then, before he could stop himself, he did exactly that.

When he put his hand on her neck, she started. Her eyes opened wide but she didn't pull away. Tox gave her enough time to do that. That one second, that's all she would have needed to back away. To pretend nothing had happened.

But instead, her eyes heated.

And that was all he needed.

He pulled her down, bringing his mouth to hers in a kiss that started hot and then blazed higher, instantly. Her mouth dragged across his. Her bottom lip—he could spend a full day right there, just running his tongue along the sensual swell and curve her mouth made.

Instead, though, she kissed him harder, her tongue meeting his, matching him in a contest of wills that had two winners. She tasted like mint and vanilla, and something that was uniquely her, something rich and warm. Heady.

Tox groaned against her mouth—and he couldn't help it, he needed more. More contact than just her lips against his. He moved his hand from behind her head to around her waist and pulled her toward him. She pulled back momentarily, her eyes wide and dilated. She teetered, off-balance.

Taking advantage of the move, Tox pulled her down so that she fell against his body.

Now she was on top of him. There was no way she wasn't going to feel how hot she was making him. He was harder than the pole at the station, and goshdarn if he didn't want another kiss from that mouth that was about to make him over-the-top crazy.

# CHAPTER 12

On top of Tox Ellis. On *top* of him. In one of her recliners, no less.

Instead of trying to figure out how to get off him, though, Grace tried to catch her breath. It wasn't easy. Tox was all man, and getting more manly by the second, she realized. She should climb down and claim a billing problem in the back. She should tell him he could settle up with the gift certificate later.

Instead, she lowered her mouth to his again. She kissed him harder, a white-hot blaze igniting in her core. She was melting inside, she couldn't think, she couldn't hear anything but his moan and a low roar of blood pounding in her eardrums. His hand strayed from her waist to the small of her back, and he pulled her flush against him.

She tried to prevent herself—she really did—but she moved against his length, driving her hips into his. He responded in kind, digging his hands into her hair and scraping his lips against hers. She couldn't breathe, not with the explosion she was feeling inside—she'd never felt heat like this in her body. It scared the wits out of Grace, and she knew one thing—she did not want to stop kissing this man whose arms felt like steel and whose tongue was hotter than sin.

Then, from the door, came a noise.

A soft, "Oh!" that should have been almost inaudible, but Grace's senses seemed super-powered, heightened almost to the point of pain. The exclamation rang like a gunshot inside her head and she jerked her mouth away from Tox and turned.

Pastor Jacobs stood in the open doorway, one hand over his mouth. In his other hand, tucked under his arm, he held what looked like a struggling animal of some kind.

Behind him, her sister Samantha was doubled over in what looked like a silent laughing fit.

"Oh, Jesus," said Grace.

"I don't think He's watching that closely right now, child," said Pastor Jacobs.

# CHAPTER 13

Grace clambered off Tox as gracefully as she could while her sister laughed behind the still-stunned looking minister. "I was..." she started. "I was just..."

Samantha made a choking noise. Grace knew that once Samantha got caught in a giggle fit, it wasn't something she could snap out of quickly, no matter how hard anyone tried to get her to calm down. And Sam had launched herself into this one full force.

"It's okay, Grace," said Pastor Jacobs.

Tox's grin wasn't helping anything, Grace noted. He looked like he'd just put out a fire one-handed.

"I was just looking for any more needles. They're so thin, and light, you know. Practically invisible. Remember when I forgot to take the one out of the top of your head, Pastor?" It hadn't been one of her finer moments, actually. Why did it always have to be the pastor who saw her do the most stupid things?

Samantha let out a giggle that sounded almost maniacal in its intensity. "I'm sorry," she said, both hands over her mouth. "It was just ... the Pastor, and the dog ... oh, stop it, the *dog* ..." And she was off again, no hope for return.

Grace said crisply, "Can you please wait on the porch for us, Samantha?"

Sam nodded and fled, still hiccupping with laughter.

Grace smoothed the front of her jeans, as if she could erase what the pastor had seen.

"You have a dog with you, I see," she said formally.

"I do," said Pastor Jacobs with relief. "I sure do. I met both the puppy and your sister on my walk over here, and I thought maybe you might know something about where this little gal belongs."

Tox by now had swung up in his chair so that he was no longer reclined. He unfolded himself and stood next to Grace. She could feel his heat against her arm. Self-consciously, she rubbed her lips on the back of her hand. No gloss transferred. Somehow she'd lost all of it against Tox's mouth. Great.

"I'm sorry," said Grace. "I've never seen her before."

Pastor's long face fell, making him look even more lachrymose than usual. "I guess I'll take her to the shelter, then."

"Wait," said Grace. "Let's at least have a good look at her."

From the porch outside, a howl of laughter rose.

Both men joined Grace in pretending they heard nothing.

Pastor Jacobs set the dog on the hardwood floor. It was small and yellow, a solid little block of short-haired fluff, with longer hair at the ears. She could have been a mix between a Golden Retriever and some kind of spaniel, with her short little legs, long body and long, fluffy ears. She was ridiculous looking. She was so thin her ribs poked out from her skin, and she was missing a patch of fur on the top of her head. A thin trail of drool went to the floor, and her eyes were wet and sad as she looked up at Grace and Tox.

Another howl of laughter went up on the porch.

"What was so funny about the dog?" Grace asked. She knew Samantha was laughing at catching her and Tox in a clinch, but she'd said something about laughing at the dog beforehand.

"I think she was laughing at me, not the dog. I'd just gotten out of a service—Bill Tunney's funeral, you know."

All three pulled appropriately somber faces. Grace had never met the man herself.

"And I was still in my robes. While I was outside saying goodbye to the mourners, this little thing came up and squatted on Mrs. Chumley's shoe. When Mrs. Chumley screamed at her, the dog ran right out into traffic. I ran after her."

Samantha's head popped up in the window that opened onto the porch. "And then he was chasing the dog! All flapping in his purple robes, that dog always just in front of him. They shut down all of Second Street. I swear, a school bus almost plowed into the Turners's tractor."

Color drained from Pastor Jacobs's face. "Can you imagine?" he whispered. "If I'd caused a devastating accident, just because I was chasing a ... dog?" The unspoken curse word hung in the room.

Samantha—still laughing—disappeared from view again.

Tox quirked an eyebrow at Grace. "Is she always like that?"

"Drunk at noon? Not really."

Pastor said, "She's not drunk." A pause while he scratched the dog on her head. "Is she?"

Grace laughed then. "No." Thank goodness.

Pastor heaved a sigh. "I guess I'll take this one down to the pound. I'd keep her myself but I promised Mrs. Jacobs I'd never bring home anything with fur that wasn't in the shape of a coat. It's too bad. She's a nice pup."

The pathetic-looking puppy was in the process of gnawing on the top of Tox's boot. It appeared to be a fruitless task—her teeth couldn't puncture the leather, but she was shining them with the copious amount of spit coming from her mouth. For a moment Grace pictured herself with the dog. Cuddling in bed ... It would be nice to have a dog keeping her warm at night.

But it wouldn't be fair when she was working long hours at the clinic, and she could never bring a dog inside, not while she had clients with extreme allergies. The animal shouldn't even be inside now.

Tox bent forward. "No need, Pastor. I'm headed that way myself."

"You are?"

"I had to go grab a couple of things at the hardware store."

Mike's Hardware was two doors down from the city pound.

"You're on your motorcycle," Grace pointed out.

He shrugged. "I'll walk."

Grace eyed the way the dog pushed herself into Tox's arms, burying her nose under his chin. Good grief, just minutes ago, she'd been the one drooling all over his body.

This was not how today was supposed to go at all.

"Are you sure you don't mind, son?"

"Nope," Tox shook his head. "I'll take her now. Grace, are we done for the day?"

Samantha's giggle rose from outside, so loud it sounded like someone was tickling her.

"Yes," said Grace. "You were a good patient."

"Stop it!" screamed Sam. "You're *killing* me."

Without acknowledging the sound, Grace shut the window with a bang. "Thanks for coming." She cleared her throat. "For coming *in*."

Tox snorted. Even the pastor gave a small smile.

Grace shook her head and glanced at the schedule on her phone. Maybe if she appeared very busy ...

"Will you go out with me?" said Tox. The puppy in his arms licked his chin.

Grace looked behind her. "Are you talking to *me*?"

"Well, I don't think it's me. On that note," said Pastor Jacobs, "I'll take my leave."

"I'll walk you out, Pastor. Grace, I just wanted to know if tomorrow night you'd go grab a bite with me. I'll come get you here. Say six?"

She looked down at the face of her phone, as if she could find something there to say. She was so surprised she could only think of one thing, only one word that might be appropriate.

"Yes."

## CHAPTER 14

The dog was a runt. A sick, tiny runt. Tox should have felt sad looking into the dog's watery eyes as he held her. He should have felt sad for the life the puppy'd had so far, and even more sadness for how she'd probably never make it, not going to a place like the Darling Bay Pound, but all he could think about was Grace's mouth on his, the warm solid softness of her as she'd fallen down on top of him. Yeah, he might have pulled her a little bit, but a bit of encouraging wasn't what got her stretched out full-length along his body.

Tox held the puppy against his chest and gave her a scratch on her belly. He smiled as she wriggled herself to an upside-down position in his arms.

Grace had said yes.

He passed Mrs. Cross and nodded to her, ignoring her dropped mouth as she registered that the thing he cradled was a puppy. A little girl holding her brother's hand in front of Skip's noticed the same thing and made a sound that could have shattered crystal.

He passed Josie's Cinnamon Rolls, and his mouth

watered. Josie was a flipping genius with sugar and flour. From inside the yellow-walled shop, she waved out at him. She was pretty. He'd dated her for a short time last year, till she realized he was more into scoring overtime at work than scoring with her. It just hadn't been a match, no matter how cute she was.

He stroked the puppy's tiny head with his thumb. But what was really cute? The warm honeyed sound Grace got in her voice after she'd been kissing him—almost a purring noise. That was cute. No, that was *hot*. Tox felt the summer sun breaking through the fog, hitting the back of his leather jacket. It would be too warm to wear it soon.

Or was that just him overheating, thinking of Grace?

Dang. She was a two-alarm fire, and he wasn't planning on dumping water on that fire. He wanted to watch her blaze, and he wanted to burn along with her.

Inside the pound, John Skinner gave him a nod as he entered. "Got a dog for me?" He sounded displeased, and his long nose wrinkled the slightest bit. Tox had known Skinner since they were kids, and even back then he wouldn't have given him a job dealing with animals. Skinner was tall and painfully thin, with a perpetual frown on his face. He had a thin mustache that made him look as if he were about to tie a girl to the railroad tracks. The funny thing was that Tox knew he was a fighter—he really *tried* to save the animals under his care. He hated putting them down, and once Tox had seen him at the bar after a rough shift. After three martinis (two too many for a guy his size), he'd started weeping into his gin about the dog he'd had to put to sleep that day.

"Give it over," said Skinner, gesturing to the counter.

All Tox had to do was let the dog go. Just fill out the form. Walk out the door.

Why then, was he having such a hard time doing it? He felt stupid for even admitting it to himself, but when he looked down, he could see Grace in this darn dog's eyes. Was it that maple color? Was it that soft, welcoming look of trust? He hadn't been looked at like that for a long time.

Now two girls in one day had looked at him that way.

"You gonna keep her or what?" Skinner crossed his arms in front of his chest. "Because I don't got all day. I got two sick dogs in the back that might not make it. They'll probably give this one what they have, even though doc's got 'em on all the antibiotics already."

Tox jerked his chin. "You talk like you don't care."

Skinner said nothing, keeping his arms crossed.

"But you do."

"Whatever. Don't bust my balls on this. You leaving the dog or taking her yourself?"

Tox hesitated. "Don't you always say it's the puppies you can adopt out, no problem?"

Skinner raised one eyebrow so high it almost got lost in his combover. "Have you looked at that mangey little thing? She's two breaths away from dead."

Tox looked down. The puppy was shaking like it was caught in a rainstorm. She was matted fur and ribcage. Drool trailed from her mouth, and her eyes ran so that it looked like she was crying. And still that little tail gave a soft *thump-thump-thump* against the leather of his jacket.

"She's a strong little pup," said Tox. The dog took the finger he gave her and chewed on it. "See? Friendly."

"She's so hungry she's trying to eat your flesh, that's all." Skinner held out his hands. "Come on, Tox."

The pup stopped chewing on his finger and looked up at him. She gave a soft whine and tilted her head to the side.

She was ugly. Little. Sick. And Tox was totally in love with her.

"Well, heck."

"Looks like you have a dog, my friend."

Tox didn't say anything, just held the puppy tight and barreled out the door he'd just come in.

He wondered if the dog would mind a short ride on a motorcycle. He held her up to his face and received another lick.

Seemed like she was pretty daring. She'd probably like it.

## CHAPTER 15

"A date? Tomorrow night?"

"Well, at least you finally stopped laughing."

Samantha rocked back on her heels and set down the African violet she was repotting on Grace's back porch. "Where are you going?"

"I don't know."

"What time?"

"That I don't know, either." Grace brushed dark soil off her hands and looked with satisfaction at the geranium she was cutting back. The sharp, acrid scent pleased her nose. It smelled like dusty summer to her. Their mother had loved geraniums. "And I don't know why I'm going out with him at all. His name is Tox, for Pete's sake. I swore after the last guy—"

"The last three guys."

"—the last three guys that I would only date someone healthy. Someone with his head on straight and his stuff together."

Samantha waved a dirty hand. "Whatever. The real question is: what are you going to wear? I have a couple college application clients tomorrow night. If I do your makeup in the morning, will you promise not to touch it all day?"

Grace felt a flutter of nerves in her stomach. "Oh, crap."

Samantha finished tamping more soil around the root ball. "Okay, we'd better get started. Pass me that watering can. And guarantee me you won't wear those shoes."

Looking down at her favorite black Dansko clogs, Grace frowned. "These are cute."

"They're birth control."

Shocked, Grace said, "Well, *good*. It's not like I'm going to need any other kind."

Finishing with the violet, Samantha said, "Look at all this mint! It's crazypants! Let's make virgin mojitos!"

"I'll pass," said Grace.

Samantha pulled off her gloves and stood. "Put down the trowel."

"I still have three more petunias to put in."

"Screw the petunias. You can't kill those things. Come inside, have a fake drink with me, and we'll decide what you're wearing."

"But ..."

"You need to loosen up a little, and you might as well start doing that tonight." Samantha went inside, the screen door slamming behind her.

"Wait a minute." Grace followed Sam inside. "What do you mean?"

Sam gave a light laugh as she rinsed the mint she'd picked. "I didn't mean anything by it. Just that you could stand to let go of the reins a little bit."

Grace felt a flash of heat. That's exactly what Gary, her last boyfriend, had said. Right before he'd dumped her to take the trip they'd planned together, absconding with her money which she could only assume he blew on the horses.

Her sister snapped her fingers in front of her. "Earth to Grace. You haven't heard a word I've been saying, have you? Drink this." She pressed a cold glass into Grace's hand. "Now, to my room. I have just the right thing for you to wear."

"I'm not looking like a hooch. You can't make me."

Samantha said, "I'm just going to take it as a compliment that you think I could come close to making you look like one."

"And no heels!" The drink did actually taste amazing. Light and sweet, tart and not too minty. "How did you make this?"

"I stared into it until the sin in my soul filled the glass. Why? You like it?"

Grace said. "It's not bad. Bring on the carnal wear."

Samantha pulled Grace into the spare bedroom. "Eye shadow! Perfume! Low-cut top! This is what I've been waiting for ever since I moved in!"

"Lucky me," Grace said, bumping Sam with her shoulder.

But in fact, she meant it.

---

THE NEXT DAY AT WORK, Grace had a hard time hiding her nerves. As Scrug Watson hung up his green Deere baseball cap on her hat rack, she'd dropped a box of clean needles with a clatter that made everyone in her treatment room jump. Scrug said, "Whatchoo nervous about, girl?"

"Accident, sorry," she'd said lightly, picking them up.

Within ten minutes she'd stubbed her toe twice and knocked over a glass of water on her desk, soaking her day planner. She told herself to breathe, but somehow taking in air and holding it made her feel even more jumpy.

By five thirty, she was out of the practice, walking home. She stumbled twice. Stupid Danskos.

By quarter to six, she was home.

Ten minutes later, she was in her bathroom, checking her makeup.

She wouldn't be nervous.

It would be stupid to be nervous.

*Jeez*, she was nervous. She felt like a jumpy cat balancing on top of a cement mixer.

The mascara her sister had insisted on putting on her this morning was still black and thick. Just like Samantha had promised, it hadn't smudged, but then again, Grace had been too terrified to touch her eyes all day. She'd flat-out refused the eye shadow after she'd read the ingredients to her sister. Sodium laurel sulfate and propylene glycol? Who knew what those did, being absorbed into the skin all day?

Now, Grace put on the deep cherry lipstick her sister had insisted she wear. She took a step back and smoothed her hair. The black V-neck was deep, but it hadn't made her feel embarrassed today as she'd leaned over patients, so it wasn't too low. The dark red straight skirt made her calves look good, she could admit that. The black heels? At least four inches high? She still hated them. Why women felt they had to ... But she'd promised Sam, and she would do this for her.

That part of the date, anyway. Samantha had also said that she should try hard to get into trouble before the end of the night.

Grace had punched her sister in the shoulder. "I'm not putting out."

"Who says that anymore? Putting out. Maybe you should stay inside with your knitting and your herbal tea."

Stung, Grace said, "I like knitting. And more tea is always good."

Samantha had just laughed and shoved two condoms into Grace's purse. Grace hadn't asked her why she had them. She didn't want to know.

The front doorbell rang.

Grace took a deep breath and tried very hard not to wobble on her way through the office and into the hallway.

Tox stood on the porch, bigger and brawnier than she'd remembered. He could probably lift a car if he had to, and someone in his profession might have to on occasion.

He'd been looking over his shoulder, but turned as the door opened.

"Oh, crap," Tox said as his face fell. "What are you wearing?"

## CHAPTER 16

As first date opening lines went, it was right up there with "What was your name again?" and "We're going Dutch, right?"

Tox's mouth seemed full of concrete. He had to find something better to say, fast—before her feelings got hurt. Well, it was probably too late for that.

Grace looked confused and then chagrined. She tugged at the neckline of her shirt as if she wanted to cover up the skin of her chest and neck. He hadn't meant *that*. She looked amazing. The outfit did all sorts of things for her deliciously hot body, and dang, did he like looking at her.

She was just going to ruin the date if she wore that, that was all.

"My sister's clothes," Grace said, stepping forward onto the porch, closing the door firmly behind her. "I told her it was a bad idea."

"Are you kidding?" Tox almost stuttered, tripping over the words. "No! I don't want you to think—well, of course you'd think ..."

"That you think I look terrible?" She put her shoulders

back, and her next words were strong. "Well, I think I look nice." She blinked hard, as if she were working on believing it herself.

Tox stepped forward and put his hands on her shoulders. "You look incredible."

"I ... what? You just said ..."

"You look hotter than the devil's kitchen. I can't believe how good you look." Didn't she *know* that?

"Oh." She bit her bottom lip. Chewed on it, really. Then she blushed. Yeah, Tox liked it when she did that. In fact, he wanted her to do that all the time. Everywhere. He wondered what she looked like she was naked and blushing. How far did that red spread?

"But you do have to change."

"Excuse me?"

"We're doing something that will require the use of sneakers. And old clothes."

An expression of relief crossed her face. "Oh, thank goodness."

"You don't mind?"

"Hang on, I'll be right back."

Tox waited on the porch. Grace had a knack for decorating, he noticed. Not like the designers on HGTV that Coin watched at the station, not all fancy, but both her practice in the old Victorian and this little house had the same feeling, as if they had grown up around her, naturally. There had to be fifty potted plants, flowers blooming and draping, all colors. Comfortable old wooden furniture—a swing and three chairs—invited him to sit. He imagined her entertaining out here, seated with her bare feet pulled up underneath her, hair loose, pouring glasses of iced tea for friends.

For a brief second, he wondered if he could ever be

someone who sat out here with her. He imagined her bare feet resting in his lap.

Grace came outside, dressed in a blue zippered sweatshirt, jeans, and blue canvas shoes. Her hair, so carefully styled before, was pulled back into a ponytail. She'd rubbed off the dark lipstick, but she still wore the prettily smudged eye makeup. She looked ready to paint a house or play paintball. How was it possible that she looked even hotter now, dressed like this?

"What are we doing?" she asked. Her face was open. Happy. Expectant.

Tox didn't want to let her down. "I'm not sure if you have an online profile, but I think it's required by law that if you do, you have to say you like long walks on the beach. So I thought we'd do that." He'd meant it as funny and tongue-in-cheek. Now that he'd said it out loud, it just kind of sounded stupid. So he added the clincher. "With my new dog."

# CHAPTER 17

He'd kept the dog!

Grace squeaked—she knew she did—when Tox led her to the dog crate leashed into the back of a black truck.

"Where's your motorcycle?"

"Turns out she doesn't like riding much. That was one exciting ride home yesterday, I'll tell you that much."

Grace grinned and climbed up on the back tire so she could reach through the crate's bars to give the wee pup a scratch. "So you own all the big boy toys? The motorcycle, the big truck ... Do you have the boat, too?"

"Does a jetski count?"

Raising one eyebrow at him, Grace decided to let him off the hook for the water sports safety lecture. Besides, the dog was taking all her attention. "Can she ride in the cab with us?"

"Whatever you want, darlin'," said Tox with an unexpected drawl that made Grace's knees get warm.

The puppy sat on Grace's lap during the short ride to Fenton's Beach. When Tox took the corner at First she almost spilled off, but then she scrambled back, seemingly desperate not to lose contact.

Tox parked in the lot and they walked past Mabel's Café toward the sand. Grace felt awkward, rejecting every sentence that came to mind as too silly or too frivolous.

Down near the water, though, the salt wind whipping her ponytail, the small dog stretching her leash to its limit, Grace felt the tightness in her jaw start to relax. "She's adorable," she said to Tox.

"I know."

"That fur, though."

"She has a grooming appointment tomorrow."

Grace nodded. "She's too skinny."

"Agreed," he said amiably. "We'll fix that right up."

"How?"

"Steak. Lots of steak."

Surprised, Grace said, "I can't imagine that would be the best diet for a puppy."

"I was teasing," he said. "Mostly. But ice cream isn't out of the question."

"Really?'

"Man, you're easy to tease."

"Gah. I've always been gullible," said Grace. She bent over and undid the laces of her shoes. "Once a guy convinced me he was the first test-tube baby in the world."

"Why would he say that?"

"I don't know." Grace had never thought to wonder why he'd done that. "I have no idea."

"Men will say anything to get laid," he said.

The sand was cool and damp between her toes. "Is that true, do you think?"

Tox's eyebrows raised as he took off his own shoes. They

left them in a companionable pile at the edge of the iceplant, safely out of the waves' way. "*Oh*, yeah."

"I don't think you're supposed to admit that on a date," said Grace.

He looked rueful. "Probably not."

Something that resembled daring filled Grace spine. "What's the worst thing you've ever said? To get laid?"

"Oh, man. I really don't think I should go there."

Her heart beat rapidly. "I'll tell you the worst thing I ever said." Grace could only think of something she'd heard her sister say at a bar.

Tox laughed. "Girls do it, too?"

The bar line Samantha had said tripped off her tongue. "I told a guy that I could tie a knot in a cherry stem with my tongue."

"I'm intrigued. You can?"

"Sure. Who can't?" Grace had never even tried. The lie burned a path into her stomach.

Tox tugged on the leash. The puppy ran toward a seagull, pretending she wasn't on leash, her short legs scrabbling at the wet sand. "Wow. But if it was the truth, then I don't think that counts as a bad thing. It's only morally reprehensible if you're making it up, just to get some action."

"A man with a conscience," Grace said, trying to will her blush to stop. "That's admirable."

"Don't say that yet. I once told a girl I'd run a baker's dozen marathons."

"And you hadn't?"

"I don't run unless it's from a bear."

A wave ran at them, and they dodged. A young woman wearing headphones race-walked past them, arms pumping. Grace said, "What kind of exercise do you do then?"

Tox looked at her with a leer.

She blushed harder. "Okay, never mind. Just get some exercise sometime, would you? It's good for you. What other lies have you told women?"

"My worst lie?"

"Yeah."

Tox guided her around a large strand of seaweed that blocked their way. "I once told a girl that I was a Russian prince."

"To get in her pants?"

He shrugged. "She was gorgeous."

Grace felt a funny twist in her stomach. She wondered what gorgeous looked like to him. Probably not jeans and a sweatshirt with hair pulled back in a scruffy ponytail. "How did you explain your lack of accent?"

"Oh, I had an accent."

"You're kidding me. Do it."

He grinned. "No way."

"*Do* it."

"Zen I vud haff to keel you."

As she dodged another wave, Grace laughed, deeply, from her belly. "So you were a German Russian?"

"I was Eastern European. Of some flavor. I was rich, and my mother owned a fleet of horses."

"Horses come in fleets?"

When he smiled, his eyes crinkled at the edges in wonderful ways. "They did for me, when I was a child in the palace. I was raised by six full-time nannies."

"How could being raised by six nannies possibly be attractive to someone?"

"I think it was the implied money that the fleet of horses and the flight of nannies that did it."

"So it worked."

He gave a nod and whistled to the dog who gave no sign of hearing him. "Totally."

"How long did it last?"

"A week."

"A good week?"

He glanced at her sideways. "Not that great. She was a little crazy."

"Crazy for falling for a Russian prince?"

"Actually, that was my out. I had to return to the land of my people."

"And you're calling *her* crazy?"

"She tried to choke my ex-girlfriend when we ran into each other at a bar."

"Oh!" said Grace. "Okay, that's crazy."

"I've never been attracted to the sane ones. The good-for-me ones."

*Me, neither.* She didn't say it. There was a pause. Grace considered filling it, but she was thrown. Everything about this man threw her. His casual good looks, his confidence, his jokes. The way she wanted desperately to brush against him. Casually. Or more.

Then Tox said, "Which is what makes you so interesting to me. That I'm so attracted to you."

Dang, he just put it out there, didn't he? Grace felt a warmth flood her. "Oh."

"I'm looking for your crazy."

She laughed, turning her face to the last of the sunlight. It would drop behind the rapidly advancing fog bank soon, and the air would cool rapidly. Three different couples wandered the same way they did, dodging into and away from the waves. They walked in silence, laughing periodically at the dog. After a few more minutes, they both turned back toward the pier companionably.

Grace finally said, "You've seen me in two different crisis modes, so you're closer than most to knowing what my crazy is like."

"And in both cases, you were trying to take care of someone else and not yourself."

"What? No, I wasn't. Not the second time. I was just trying to breathe."

He raised an eyebrow. "You were taking care of your sister, doing everything you could do to make her think you were okay. Then you were helping me, getting the guys out to me with the baby."

"Hey," said Grace, remembering. "Why did that firefighter call you the Angel of Death? Doesn't seem like that's a very firefighter-like thing to say."

Tox's green eyes went darker, the color of the water at the edge of the foam. "Just a nickname."

"Like Tox?"

"Worse. Some people ... It just seems like bad stuff happens around me, that's all. If a call's going to go south, I'm usually either there or on my way to it."

"Huh." She wondered briefly what that meant about his relationships. "But you're a helper. You help. That's your job."

"Same as you. That's what we do, right?"

"Well." She shrugged. "If that's true at all, it's only because it's easier."

"I think that's your crazy."

"Taking care of people?" She pointed at the dog, still straining on her leash. "Number one, pot, meet kettle. And number two, that's not such a bad problem to have." She had to change the subject. This was too much, too intimate. "What are you going to name her?"

"I'm not sure."

"What's in the running?"

He shortened the leash as an errant wave threatened to drench the puppy. "I like Loki."

"No," said Grace without hesitation.

"Why not?"

"She's a girl! And Loki was the god of destruction. It's like naming your kid Damien. You get what you deserve."

"Okay. Then Appaloosa."

"That's the opposite of Loki, I guess, but that's so long. And wouldn't you shorten it to Loose? Then she'd be guaranteed to be pregnant before she even graduates her first training class."

"Methyl."

"Ethyl?"

He slowed his pace, and then stopped, slapping his thigh. The dog came running. Heck, Grace wanted to, too. "No, Methyl. It's a hazmat thing."

"It's short for some chemical?"

"Yep."

Why wasn't he just saying what it was short for? "And ..."

"Methyl-ethyl bad stuff. Only ... we don't normally say the word stuff."

"Ah."

"You know the rule of thumb for methyl-ethyl bad stuff?"

Grace shook her head. His voice was teasing again, and she liked the way it sounded in her ears. Rough and happy.

He held up a fist, his thumb up, holding his arm out straight toward the horizon. "Imagine there's an explosion out there, way out at sea."

Squinting, she said, "Okay."

"You want to stay far enough away from the methyl-ethyl bad stuff that when you hold up your hand like this, your thumb covers it up." He looked at her, and then, to her surprise, he put his arm around her waist and drew her against his chest. "It's pretty technical."

"I can tell," she laughed, breathless. "You must have gone to school a long time for that."

"I put in at *least* six hours of training. Can I kiss you now?"

"Again," she said. "You did that once already."

He smiled. "And it's all I've been able to think about doing ever since."

She reached up on tiptoe to kiss him.

Grace thought it would be a light kiss, like the moment. A sweet kiss. On the beach, in the sunset, in a handsome firefighter's arms, what could be nicer?

But the kiss wasn't nice. Or, at least, it wasn't for long. His mouth, soft at first, soon blazed against hers. The heat of it stunned her, lighting every cell in her body on fire. His tongue was firm, direct, sure. He tasted like mint and something darker. His hands held her close, tightly, so that she could feel his arousal. He said her name against her kiss, so that the wind tore it away.

Grace felt something at her ankle.

Something insistent, even more so than Tox's kiss.

Methyl was humping her shoe. "Oh, *come* on, dog!" She shook her leg out of Methyl's grasp and ignored Tox's laughing. "Really? How did you train your dog to do this already?"

Tox drew Grace close again. "She joost feels zuh passione."

Bumping her hip against his, she turned so that she could look out at the ocean, hoping to catch her breath. To draw herself back in line. No man should affect her like this.

She felt thrown, off kilter. It was a foreign feeling, and she wasn't sure she liked it.

"I thought you were supposed to put out fires," she said, not looking at him. "Not start them."

His lips were at her ear. "I'm an arsonist when it comes to you."

Grace wheeled, pulling from his arms. "That's the worst line I've ever heard." She pointed at the pier ahead of them. "Are we headed back there to eat?"

"Yep."

"Race you." She ran. Somehow, she knew he'd let her get ahead.

But she knew he was right behind her. She wanted nothing more than for him to catch her. And at the same time, she knew he wasn't right. *Toxic.*

A terrible idea.

A hot, terrible, intoxicating idea.

She ran harder.

CHAPTER 18

Grace, since the kiss on the beach, had kept him at arm's length, and Tox wasn't sure what he'd done wrong.

Surreptitiously, he blew into his hand. Breath, check. Still minty from the gum he'd chewed on the way to her house. He remembered putting on his deodorant before he left the house, so that wasn't it.

Maybe he was a terrible kisser. Maybe he'd horrified her with a bad kiss! Oh, no. Could that be it? He'd never had any complaints in that area, but there was always a first time.

But then again, she'd accused him of starting a fire. And that had to be a good thing, right?

They'd tucked Methyl safely into her crate, locking the door. She drank water and promptly passed out in a sandy heap.

Now they sat facing each other at one of the picnic tables Darling Bay had installed two years before. Tox had never taken the time to sit here before. It was pretty great, actually. The view of the breakers was impressive from up here on the raised sidewalk—they could watch not only the water crashing, but the surfers being thrown over the waves, as if the ocean was shaking them out like a damp towel.

"How's your burger?" he asked.

"Terrible," Grace said, but she took another big bite.

"I can tell you hate it." Tox opened the bun and added more salt from the paper packet. "Hey, look, there's Lexie."

Lexie strolled next to an older man who was dressed in a blue polo that paunched out at his round belly. It couldn't have been a date—he looked at least twenty-five years older than she was. Lexie leaned down and said something to the man and then skittered toward them, leaving him standing at the top of the stairs that went down to the sand.

Lexie raced toward them, draping herself over the end of their picnic table. "Yes," she said, "before you ask, I'm on a date. I'm on a date that I got online, and right after this I'm going to go home, eat a package—no, a *crate*—of Oreos while in the tub, and then drown myself."

Grace said, "You sure you don't want to dump him right now and join us?"

Tox said, "Yeah. You wanna? Hey, wait." Was his own date going so badly Grace wanted her friend to join them? But then Grace dropped a quick wink at him, and he remembered the way she'd responded to him on the beach. He took another look at the man standing by the steps. His thinning hair was almost in a combover because of the wind. Tox could have some compassion for the guy.

"Nah," said Lexie. "I just want you both to get a good look at him so that if I go missing, you'll know whose basement to tear up. His name is Scooter Fuzz."

"It is *not*," said Grace.

Lexie held up a hand. "Swear. He showed me his license. Okay, I have to go so I can get this over with faster.

Enjoy your burgers." She waggled her eyebrows and was gone.

Tox took her advice and took another big bite out of his burger. Around it, he managed to say, "Thish is amashing."

Grace shook her head and held up her hamburger to the sunset streaking across the sky. "Neither of us should be eating this. Think of the gluten in the bun, the fat in the burger, and that's not even to mention how processed the bacon is. And this cheese! This isn't cheese. It's melted plastic." She glared at it. Then her face softened. "Delicious, delightful, addictive melted plastic."

"That's what I'm talking about. And hey, this is a step up for me? You know how times I eat McDonalds a week?"

"Don't tell me." She meant it.

"I throw some Carls Jr. in there if I'm feeling like I need a little something better. This, this is highbrow cuisine. Lettuce and everything. Have a fry."

"No, thanks," she said, but her fingers lingered near his fry basket. "I'm happy with my salad on the side."

"Which you haven't touched yet."

"I will."

"No, you won't," Tox said. He nudged the fries closer to her. "Because you want some of these."

"No way. I want to live to be a hundred."

"Potatoes. They're a vegetable."

Her hand skittered toward the fries and then away. "No ..."

"I won't tell anyone."

"That's not the point," she said. She had a tiny dab of mustard just below her lip, and he wanted to lick it off.

"What's the point, then?"

She put down the french fry she'd picked up, placing it squarely back in its paper basket. They both looked at the squabbling seagulls next to the table who were fighting over half a dropped corn dog.

"This isn't real food," she said, but she didn't sound convinced.

"Look," Tox said, opening his burger bun again. "Meat. Vegetables. Wheat. Pretty straightforward food to me. You're sad it's not a tofu burger? Because we can go get you one of those. They have 'em down the block."

"No!" She gripped her burger tighter and took another bite.

"I didn't think so."

Grace chewed and watched the waves. She was so all-fired cute, with that ponytail and that earnest expression. She'd gone somewhere, far away, and he wasn't sure how to get her back.

"Give yourself a break, huh?"

She jumped. "What?"

"I know when someone's beating themselves up, and that's what you're doing. Just enjoy your burger, huh?"

She bit her bottom lip, then licked away the mustard. He missed it as soon as it was gone. "I'm fine."

Sure. She could play it that way. Tox wasn't that big on pushing anyone, anyway.

A little boy wandered past the table, his mother right behind him. She was on her cell phone, looking into the parking lot, and didn't notice the little boy had let go of the string of his yellow balloon. Tox lunged sideways, grabbing it while it was still a few feet over his head. "Hey! Here you go, kid."

The mother thanked him as she tied the string around the child's wrist.

When he sat back down, Grace said, "That was nice."

"All in a day's work. Helium's deadly, you know."

She laughed again. "Yeah. That's why every kid in America sucks it as often as possible."

Tox smiled gamely. Helium was actually a great way to kill yourself, too, and he'd been on enough of those calls over the years that he had a hard time forgetting that.

"Whoa," Grace said. "Where did *you* go?"

"Sorry." He jerked himself back to the conversation. Normal people didn't think things like that. He always forgot. "It's just …"

"Just what?"

Tox met Grace's eyes. She looked at him like she really wanted to know what he was thinking. Like it meant something, the next thing he said. And instead of saying what he was thinking—that nothing mattered anyway, that nothing good lasted—he said, "It's just that you should really have one of these fries. They're the best on the coast."

"Well, okay, then," Grace said. Her voice was happy, and the look on her face as she closed her eyes matched.

He didn't want to be anywhere else.

Then the car crashed into the pier behind Grace.

# CHAPTER 19

G race felt, rather than heard, the noise.

A cacophony of sound—screams, guttural cries for help—split the air.

Tox who'd been facing the accident, was up and running before Grace had even fully turned around in her seat.

A small black car—expensive looking with custom rims, the kind rich tourists drove through town—had broken through the pier's barrier and had driven at least fifty feet down the pier before hitting the rail, smashing partially through it. The car was balanced, teetering. It looked as if a strong wind might blow it all the way off and down to the water below. Inside, Grace could see that the airbags had deployed but it was impossible to tell how many people were still in the car.

People were running toward the crash, but Tox moved faster than anyone else. He stopped to check a woman who was bleeding from the face. He said something to her, and flagged another person down. Grace heard him say, "Direct pressure. Keep it there," and then he ran to the car.

From inside the vehicle came a sharp scream.

Tox turned around and looked right at Grace, and somehow, she knew.

"Samantha," she breathed, and then Grace was running, too, faster than she ever knew she could, straight down the pier. The car had struck several people, and she didn't care about their injuries. They didn't matter.

Only getting to the car mattered.

"You're going to help me," said Tox.

His words didn't matter, either. "Sam! Samantha!" Grace could see her sister's hair, her head at a strange angle in the front seat. The driver—whoever he was—looked as if he was waking up, turning his head in confusion.

"Grace!" barked Tox. "I need you." A piece of the pier, part of the railing, broke off next to his elbow and sailed downward, toward the crashing waves.

Grace's hand rested on the glass of the passenger window, as close as she could get to her sister. "Okay. Anything. Tell me," she said. The lower part of the door was warped, the handle sheared off by hitting something. How would they ever ...

Tox touched her arm. His hand was warm. Reassuring. As if everything was okay, which it obviously wasn't. "We need to secure the car. I don't want anyone to come near it, I don't trust the weight." As if listening to him, the pier gave an ominous creak below their feet. "I need you to keep them back." He gestured at the crowd gathering.

But Grace couldn't do that. "No. I'm getting her out." She turned her head to yell through the glass. "You hear that, Sam? We're getting you out!" She pulled on the handle of the back passenger door of the car.

"Don't touch anything!" warned Tox, grabbing her hand.

"Tox—"

He pointed at the front, where the bumper was hanging treacherously over the water. "If we shift the load, we could send it right off. The water isn't deep enough here, and it'll go ass-deep in the sand ten feet under, trapping them. We won't be able to get them out in time, not if they can't get themselves out."

Grace looked at her sister's head, still unmoving.

"The only thing we can do is keep the car as still as possible. I'm going to the other side to talk to the driver, to get him not to move. Do you know who he is?"

"Not a clue." Some loser? Some dealer? Samantha had been doing so *well*, too.

A man wearing a yellow t-shirt approached her, his hands out, face pale. "What can I do?"

"Keep everyone away. Keep them back," said Grace. She swiveled her head, moving between looking at Tox and her sister. Tox was doing a great job of keeping the driver calm. Over the crashing of the waves and of the crowd, she couldn't hear his words, but the man was nodding slowly at whatever he was saying.

"The fire department will be here soon," she said to the man who wanted to help. "Can you go out and direct them? Move people out of the way and make sure they can get through."

Looking pleased to be put to use, the man pushed his way through the crowd, waving his hands. "Make way! Out of the way!"

Grace felt the planks rumble beneath her feet.

Tox looked over the top of the sedan. "The pier's unstable. Getting them back isn't enough. Get everyone all the way off."

"And leave Sam?" Grace shook her head. She'd hold the car up here with her own two hands if she had to.

"Grace, I need you to do this. I know you can do this."

"I know I can *do* it," she snapped. "That's not the issue. I'm not leaving my sister."

"I'm with her," he said. She could barely hear him over the roar of blood in her ears. "I'm not going anywhere. I need you to get back. Get them all off the pier. Make sure they're safe."

If it had been anyone else but Tox, she never would have done it. Grace knew she probably would have broken the back window and crawled inside the vehicle, no matter its instability, and stayed with Samantha. If the car had crashed down from the pier, at least she would have been inside it with the person she loved the most in the world. Holding her hand as they both died.

But Tox was right. None of them were safe, and what in the world would it do to Samantha if she woke up in the hospital just to find out her sister had been stupid, dying in an accident with strangers, an accident that could have been prevented.

The pier gave another baleful creak.

"Everyone, back!" Grace yelled in her loudest voice, the one she hadn't use since she'd captained the crew team in college. It had the same effect as it had then. People's eyes snapped to her and they did what she said. "The pier might go, we need you off." The man in yellow who had wanted to help raced to the far end of the pier to herd those tourists past the wreck to safety. Grace had to physically take a video camera out of a father-of-four's hands. "*Go!*"

The first engine made the turn onto First Street, followed by a fire truck and a red SUV. The sirens wailed, matching the sound Grace heard in her blood.

From the safety of the concrete sidewalk, Grace kept her eyes on the car. The front wheels had stopped their mid-air spin, and even though she heard the pier groan, Grace felt that if she concentrated hard enough, she could keep it standing with the will of her mind. How many times had she saved Samantha that way in the past? On long nights after Sam had failed to come home? That one time she hadn't called in a month because she'd been taken to Mexico on a lark by some rich guy's drug-dealing son? She'd been okay then. It had to work one more time.

Tox had the flat of his hand on the car's roof, somehow able to wait patiently for his backup. He looked relaxed, as if he was just chatting to the guy in the car about the beautiful sunset that was dropping behind him. Then he met Grace's eyes. He smiled slightly and nodded.

Grace's knees went wobbly, and she sat on the ground hard, cross-legged. She closed her eyes for a second, imagining the air solidifying, holding up Samantha. Holding up Tox.

After they'd extricated Samantha—still unconscious—and the man with the dark hair in the driver's seat, Grace grabbed her sister's hand and refused to let go, even when they were inserting her IV. Even when the car—now mercifully unoccupied—took a slow, dramatic header into the water below, taking a large section of the pier with it, she didn't let go of Samantha.

One of Tox's coworkers told Grace she couldn't ride in the ambulance. Grace just looked at him and then stepped around him, pulling herself up into it, sitting on the bench seat next to Samantha. Tox got in behind her.

As the ambulance rolled with lights and sirens, Grace prayed—again, harder this time—that her sister would be okay.

She knew that when she had time to think about it, she'd be grateful for Tox being next to her. She'd be so grateful for his warmth next to her, his strength, the solid bulk of him. As the ambulance raced around a corner, she was pressed into his side.

Tox's arm went around her, tightly.

"The dog!" Grace gasped. "Methyl! In the back of your truck, in her crate!"

"Sims Madigan is taking her to my house. He knows where I keep the key. Don't worry about her." Tox pressed a kiss against her temple. "Just keep holding Samantha's hand, just like you're doing. You're doing great, honey. Don't let go of either of us, okay?"

She wouldn't. No.

Grace held on.

## CHAPTER 20

In the hospital, six hours later, Samantha woke up. Grace burst into tears as soon as her sister's eyes opened, and so did Samantha. Sam dashed her hands at her face. "I don't know why I'm crying. Where am I?"

Grace tried to answer, to choke back her tears, and was astonished to find that she couldn't say anything. Her voice got stuck in her throat and she coughed.

Samantha pulled at the bedclothes and looked, wild-eyed, to Tox. "Does she need the inhaler? Can you give it to her again?"

Grace shook her head.

Tox stepped forward, putting his hand on the rail of Samantha's hospital bed. "She's fine. I think Grace is upset about you, that's all. You were in a car accident."

"The car—" gasped Grace "—it fell. Into the ocean. The car you were in fell into the *ocean.*"

Samantha's eyes widened. "How's Justin?"

"Who cares about Justin?" said Grace, feeling anger settle into her bones. Her sister was doing it again. Falling for some loser who would end up hurting her, or worse.

"You almost *died.* You came so close to death. How can I—" she broke off and turned her face away, looking at the ugly green privacy curtain. Her sister was injured. They could hash this out later. It wasn't important now.

In a calm voice, Tox said, "Justin's going to be okay. He's in surgery right now for internal bleeding but the doctor told me before they went in that it looked like a clean fix."

Samantha glanced down at her body in the bed. "I hurt. But I don't know where ..."

"You got pretty smashed up," said Tox. He gestured at her face. "You're going to be black and blue for a couple of weeks. You were out for a while. But the doctor couldn't find evidence of bleeding or broken bones. You're staying overnight to make sure they're right and to make sure you don't have a concussion."

"*What?*"

Grace took a deep breath and tried to keep it level. Neutral. She didn't want her terror—or her anger—to come through. "We were there. At the pier."

Sam's eyes brightened. "Oh! On your date!"

Oh, sometimes she looked so like Mom that it hurt Grace's heart. Especially when she was bruising like this, Grace realized. At the end of their mother's life, her face had almost always looked just the same, puffy and mottled.

"How was it?" Sam glanced at Tox, her grin wide. "Okay, tell me later. But I can't wait to hear."

Grace felt the blush spread across her face.

Tox fiddled with the bed rail. "You gotta make sure these are secure."

"I'm not a baby. I'm not going to roll out in the middle of the night. Oh, my gosh," said Samantha. "You're *both* turning red."

"Let's just put it this way," said Tox. "It was the most

exciting date I've ever been on. And technically, I think we're still on it."

"Oh!" said Samantha in delight.

"Sam! He means it was exciting because we almost watched you die."

"Oh." Sam's eyes were downcast again. "Was anyone else hurt?"

"No one critically. Some bumps and bruises." *Who is the driver?* The words sat on the tip of Grace's tongue, but she bit them back.

There was a soft knock at the door. An extremely tall firefighter with a head of bushy brown hair entered. "Hey. We were picking up a backboard the medics left, and I wanted to check on the patient."

Samantha said softly, "Hank, hi."

And as Grace watched, fascinated, her sister turned into someone else. Her color—under the bruising—went soft pink. This wasn't the same Hank Samantha had dated a long time ago, when she was taking classes at the local junior college, was it? That guy had been geeky. Skinnier than a needle in her clinic. This man, though, had the muscle to balance his height. He looked like a professional football player.

Tox bumped fists with the man. "'Sup, Hank?"

"This is what you get for taking a day off, huh?"

Tox said, "It was fine until I viewed the collision on the pier."

"You were there? Accidentally? Man, they don't call you the crap magnet for nothing, huh?" Hank turned to Samantha. "You okay?"

"Yeah," said Samantha in that same soft voice.

Grace leaned forward. "I'm her sister. Grace. I think we met once ..."

"Oh, yeah," said Hank.

But he barely looked at her.

Grace stared. She remembered loving that her sister had finally been dating someone normal. He'd been going for his fire science degree. He hadn't been a drug dealer or a gambler, a nice change of pace. Once, when Samantha was living in Florida, she'd dated a dirty cop, for heaven's sake. Or at least that's what she'd told Grace on the phone, which meant the reality might have been even worse. This guy, Hank, had been nice. Grace couldn't remember what had happened to end things.

"Anyway. You have my cell."

Sam had Hank's cell number? Her sister was full of surprises today, and this guy was the only nice surprise so far.

"Call me if you need anything." Hank paused, tugging on his ear. "Anything at all."

"As long as he's not on shift," Tox said.

"Hey, I'm on shift now," said Hank. "I'll make the guys get in the rig with me, even if you just need ice cream."

There it was again, Grace noticed. That pretty pink coloring. Yeah, there was so much she needed to talk to her sister about.

Samantha yawned.

But the time for talk wasn't now. "Okay, boys," she said, shooing them like chickens with her hands. "Out, out. She needs rest."

Tox rubbed his neck and frowned. "You're right. We're out of here. Feel better."

Grace kissed Samantha's cheek and told her she'd see her first thing in the morning. "You're all right here? Because I'll stay if you're not."

"No, I just want to sleep. I'm halfway there already."

Sam yawned again and waggled her fingers at them as they left. From the doorway, Grace blew her a kiss, just like their mother always had.

Sam smiled sleepily and caught it, pressing it to her cheek.

In the hallway, Grace wobbled.

"Whoops, sit down for a minute," said Tox, grabbing at her upper arm.

She shook him off. "I'm fine. I just ..." She just what? Just realized how close she had come to losing her last remaining blood relation? The person she loved the most? "No, I want to go home."

Hank was already striding down the hallway toward another firefighter, raising his hand in a wave.

Tox nodded, keeping his hand at her elbow. "Good. I think it's time. Let's go."

For a moment, just for a second, Grace had forgotten their date, and the fact that technically, they were still on it. "Your truck. It's still at the pier." They'd ridden to the hospital, both of them, in the back of the ambulance.

"Crap. Hang on."

Ten minutes later, Grace had taken a ride on the engine. It was completely different from the ride in the ambulance—the engine was utilitarian inside. She sat in an empty jumpseat, and they'd put a headset over her ears so she could hear them talking to each other over the roar of the engine. The four men chatted about something shift-related that she didn't follow, something about the mandations imminent on B-shift. She tuned them out and looked out the small window next to her, watching the world stare at the fire engine as they passed by. It felt like being a celebrity, the way people waved at them. Also over the headset, she heard a woman's voice say something about a medical on Turk Street.

She pushed the button they'd shown her to talk. "Don't you all have to go to the medical before they drop us off?"

Hank, sitting in the jumpseat opposite her, laughed. "That's for Engine 3. If we'd been dispatched on that, you would be holding on for dear life, what with Luke driving today. And you'd be thanking your stars that Tox was back there with you. He's the worst driver of all of us."

"Hey!" Tox said and thumped Hank on the arm with a closed fist. Hank flipped him off.

Grace felt something jolt through her—she was sitting next to Tox. In a fire engine. Her sister was alive, alive, *alive*, and she would be fine. She looked out at the line of the ocean, where the water met the sky miles away, and the expanse of it, the whitecapped beauty, made her laugh out loud with joy. "Can you turn the siren on?"

Hank shook his head. "Wish I could, but it's not allowed unless we're running a code three call."

Tox put his hand to his headphone. "What's that? Did dispatch just send us to a car fire?"

Grace hadn't heard anything in her ears.

"Hit it, Luke."

In the driver's seat, Luke whooped and the siren matched him. The engine roared as it sped up. If Grace peered carefully around the huge driver's seat she was hidden behind, she could see cars in front of them, pulling obediently over. She laughed again, and next to her, Tox's grin looked like it must be hurting his head, he was smiling so hard.

*What if someone pulled out in front of them? What if they scared someone into having a heart attack? What if the engine's brakes failed?*

Tox grabbed her hand and squeezed it, and Grace's happiness built again into joy that fizzed right up into her brain.

Then Luke shut it down. The engine slowed. At the pier, they turned into the parking lot at a decorous speed.

"That's weird," said Tox. "I could have sworn I heard something about a car fire."

"Yup," said Hank.

"Yup," said Luke.

That hadn't been safe. Or prudent. Anyone could have accidentally pulled out in front of the speeding engine. There could have been a deadly collision. Anyone could have been hurt.

But there hadn't been a crash. No one got hurt. It had turned out okay.

Grace took a breath. "Yup," she said.

## CHAPTER 21

Tox walked Grace to her front door. He should be thinking about how badly the date went. It had almost been—but not quite—the worst case scenario. He should be thinking about making sure Grace felt calm. Secure. Safe.

Why, then, couldn't he stop thinking about getting another one of those kisses? Jesus, not since he was sixteen had he been so unable to stop thinking about a woman's mouth. Grace's was perfect, and right now it was smiling at him ...

Tox rubbed his neck. "So."

"Is that still bothering you?"

"Nah," he lied.

"Come in. I can massage it for you." She went beet-red the instant the words left her mouth.

Tox grinned, but didn't say anything. He followed her in, keeping an eye on the way her rear end looked in those old jeans of hers: compact, round, so incredibly hot.

Inside, she asked him if he wanted a cup of tea. Tox

found the fact that her voice cracked adorable. "No, thanks."

"Okay, then," she said. "Sit there, on the couch." She pointed to a small red loveseat. "I'll make some. Hibiscus Rose okay?"

She'd obviously missed that he'd declined. And hibiscus rose sounded like something his grandmother would have put behind her ears. "Just fine."

She went into the kitchen. He could hear her moving around, opening cupboards, turning on the faucet. Putting his hands behind his head to alleviate some of the pressure on his neck, he leaned back and looked around.

It was just like her in here. If a plane had dropped him anywhere in the world, he would have been able to tell that he was near Grace Rowe. It smelled like her, sweet, with a hint of spice, as if she tucked packets of cinnamon and cloves in the furniture. A faint scent of something earthier, maybe incense. That wouldn't have surprised him.

The walls were painted in earth-tones, a rich russet on one wall, a dark adobe orange on another. The furniture was comfortable. Nothing fancy. Things like this red sofa, and the two oversized green chairs, things that called out to be sunk into, rested upon. There was no art, as he would have called it, on the walls. Instead, *things* hung from nails and hooks. A large drum with a fringe of feathers and beads hung on one wall. Next to the brick fireplace was a collection of what looked like painted gourds.

Hippie stuff. The kind of furnishings he would have mocked only days ago. In here, though, it looked good, like he was sitting inside some Western decorating magazine.

There was something hung above a low blue bookcase that looked like a round box made of metal. A tiny dollhouse? He stood and moved to get closer to it. Not a dollhouse, it was an aluminum open case that held a picture of a saint that had been painted with ... glitter?

"My tin *nicho*," Grace said from behind him. In her hands she held two orange mugs of tea. She'd taken off her canvas beach shoes and her bare feet surprised him, somehow. They looked so vulnerable.

"Pink toenails," he said rather stupidly.

She laughed. Such a pretty sound that was. It was like the sound of dancing. Then she said, "It's my own little, um ... do you know what a hope chest is?"

"Not really."

"It's something a girl had in the old days. She filled it with the things she made to take with her into marriage. Her hopes."

Tox felt his eyebrows shoot upward. "This is your marriage box?"

"*No.* Only the hopes for my life."

"That looks like a saint or something." He pointed at a picture glued inside. "Is that you?"

She nudged his shoulder with her own, only she was so much shorter than he was, she really just touched his elbow. His arm ached, suddenly, to go around her, but he held himself back.

"Of course not. That's just a generic saint I cut out of a magazine."

"I'm pretty sure that's blasphemous to someone. Somewhere."

"Nah," she said easily. "I just think there's something good and amazing and strong and wonderful in all of us, and part of our job here is to find out what that is."

Did she really believe that? That people were inherently good? "Well, you haven't seen the dregs of humanity, then."

She touched her lips. He wanted to do that. Badly.

"Maybe," she said. "But I've seen more than I would have liked to have seen. My first acupuncture job was in an alcoholic rehab center."

"Okay." He paused. "Maybe you've seen a little bit, then. What's with the saint, then?"

She said, sounding a bit abashed, "She kind of looks like me. A little bit, I mean. Around the nose, maybe."

Heck, she was right. Now that she said it, he could see it. It was as if they'd modeled the whole image on her. The same long toffee-colored hair that curled at the ends —always looking like it had just been caught in a windstorm. And the same big, brown eyes, as light as her hair. Almost clear, really. As expressive as the sun setting at twilight.

"My sister actually pointed it out to me in the magazine. I thought she was full of it, but I was ... I was in a low place, then. Relationship-wise. Later, I dug the magazine out of the recycling and cut it out. Look, even the same dimple."

Tox longed to touch that dimple with the very tip of his finger. Instead, he shoved his hand in his pocket.

"I used glitter glue on her dress, or robe, whatever it is. The thimble was my mother's, and it reminds me that needles have always been important in our family. After my father died, before she got sick, she took care of both me and my sister as a single mother on just the income she made as a seamstress."

There was pride in her voice, a stubbornness that he liked. And recognized. "What's the matchbook for?"

She made a murmuring sound in the back of her throat, as if she was trying to decide what, or how much, to tell him. "It's ... to remind me of something."

"And is that ..."

"A piece of chain-link fence? Yeah." Grace straightened her back. "It is."

Tox hated it when anyone pushed him, so he wouldn't do it to her. "I get it." He accepted the mug of tea from her. "Thank you for this."

They sat on the red loveseat. She was so dang close that if he moved an inch their legs would tangle. Just one inch, and they'd be touching. He wanted that so much. But she was like a kid who had called 911 after learning about it in school—all jumpy, jangled nerves. If he moved too fast, he thought she might scream, and that would seriously kill his chances of scoring another kiss from that luscious mouth.

Did she really not know how she was affecting him? Grace drew her legs up and rested the mug on her knee. She sighed and faced forward.

Her body language read as defensive. "Hey, Grace."

She started. "Yeah?"

"This tea is good."

She smiled. "I'm glad you like it."

"We don't have to do anything else."

"What?"

He knew she was only pretending confusion. "I mean it. Yeah, I loved making out with you at the beach. You're so hot I can barely look at you sometimes. You *do* something to me. And I like it. A whole lot."

"Oh." Her voice, again, was small, but that little smile stayed on her face.

"But you're spooked," Tox went on. "And I hope to all heck it's not me doing that, but if it is, I want to make it clear that all I want from you at this exact moment is this here cup of tea."

She stared at the wall behind his head, where the *nicho* hung. She bit her lower lip again. It wasn't that she was shy

—Tox would never have called her that. She was scared of something.

That was fine. As long as it wasn't him.

"There was this guy." Grace said. "That's the matchbook."

"He was an arsonist?"

"He burned me. The matchbook is to remind me not to let it happen again."

Tox set the mug down on the coffee table. He held out his hands and looked at them. "Sugar, we might have a problem. Because it's hard for me not to light a match when it's in my fingers."

## CHAPTER 22

Grace made a noise that was between a choke and a cough.

Tox was worried immediately. "How's your breathing?"

"Fine. I'm fine. It's just that sometimes you ..."

"What?"

"You make me so nervous." Grace closed her eyes, and Tox stared at the way her long lashes played against her cheeks. "I've screwed up so many times before. It's embarrassing. I'm supposed to be the healthy one, and ..."

"You don't have to tell me," Tox said. She could keep her secrets. After all, he wanted to keep his. No way would he tell her about his worries that his neck was going to put him out on medical. That he'd lose the job that meant everything to him if he didn't somehow fix it. That without the job, he was nothing. A nobody. A failure.

Yeah, Tox wouldn't push her.

"No, I want to tell you about him."

"Matchbook guy."

"I was with him a long time. Four years. It was my longest relationship."

"I've never made it past two."

"I hadn't either, until him. I thought he was the one."

"Your first real love?"

She shook her head, her hair skimming one eye. It was almost amber in the light of the orange lamp, and for a second Tox imagined sweeping it back over her shoulder. He clenched the mug tighter.

"No. I'd been in love before. I have no problem falling in love." Grace smiled again, a real one. A wide smile, and she directed it right at him. Tox felt something in his chest tighten.

She went on, "I love falling in love. I'm good at it. The problem was, I've never been good at picking the guys. One was an alcoholic, and I didn't know until he didn't call me for three weeks because he was in freaking rehab."

"You didn't know?"

"I'm clueless. That's the whole problem." She sighed and took a sip of her tea. "Another had a gambling problem. He stole the little bit of jewelry my mother left me and sold it to bet on his ponies. I almost killed him for that. And again, I didn't see it coming."

Tox's fist curled into a ball. He'd like to get his hands on that guy. "That must have hurt."

"Nothing like the four-year guy, though. I thought I'd finally done it right. Picked a guy who was healthy. Strong. He was a yoga teacher, for Pete's sake. We met when he came in for a tune-up. Nothing wrong with his body, he just wanted to make sure he was in alignment." Grace's eyes were far away. "He swept me off my feet. Told me I was beautiful."

"You are." He couldn't help it.

Grace said, "Oh!" She looked startled. And pink, so

prettily flushed. Tox had never wanted to kiss anyone so much in his whole life.

Then she went on, as if he hadn't spoken. "He told me that I was everything he was looking for. He'd been with a bunch of screwed-up people, too. He'd gotten taken in by a woman who'd turned out to be a coke-head, and he hadn't even noticed her using. We congratulated ourselves on finding someone healthy. Someone not crazy or screwed up or mean. Every year on our anniversary, we'd toast each other for not being insane."

"So what did he end up being? A sex-addict?"

Her mouth dropped open and she turned to face him, crossing one ankle under her knee. "Do you know him? Tim Smith? Oh, please tell me you don't know him."

"It was the only thing on your list of losers you hadn't mentioned."

"Sex-addict." Grace almost spat the words. "I can handle that people have problems with alcohol and drugs. I believe those are diseases, and that it's hereditary. But he tried to tell me that sex-addiction ran in his family."

"What he meant was that he saw his father cheating on his mother his whole life and had learned it was the only thing to do."

"Holy cow," she said. "Yep. That's it exactly."

Tox felt as if he'd gotten an A on a test.

"And the worst part was that I'd missed it entirely. Again. It was like my eyes were so open, and I was so happy that I was in something healthy that I completely didn't believe any of the warning signs. He would come home late and say that he was working."

"As a yoga instructor."

"Yeah." She laughed humorlessly. "I knew his studio

closed at nine, and I believed him when he said he was doing paperwork. Paperwork! Until one in the morning. He was helping someone with her poses all those nights, and I found out later it was always a different someone. So I guess he was working, all right."

"How did you find out?"

Grace set the mug on the low yellow coffee table in front of them and covered her face with her hands. "That was the worst part." She peeked at him through her fingers. "He told me."

"He *told* you?"

"He said he had to come clean before he asked me to marry him. He wanted it to be perfect between us, and nothing would do but total honesty. And the funny thing was, he thought I would be proud of him."

"He sounds like a dog."

Grace sat bolt upright and stared at him. "Methyl. You have to go home."

Tox held out his phone. "Sims sent a message. He's sleeping on the couch with her tonight. Look at this."

The picture was darling, a tuckered-out yellow puppy curled into a ball on a blue pillow. Grace held out a finger as if she could touch the dog from her seat. "Okay, good."

"So yoga-dude."

"Was awful. It was all terrible. And the worst part was that even as I prided myself for being strong and healthy, and helping other people recover, I couldn't seem to do it."

"You were in love with him," Tox said. He wasn't that fond of what he felt inside when he said it.

"That's the weirdest part," said Grace. "I was. But I realized the person I loved had never existed, and it was more like mourning a death, in a way. I'd been with him for four years, and I'd never had the foggiest idea who he was."

"But did you have fun?" Tox hated the question even as he knew he had to ask it.

"Yeah," she said slowly. "We did. That was a good part."

He wondered if they'd had good sex. And if so, was it merely good, or was it great? He stood, setting his mug next to hers, needing to move around, distribute some of the tension that ached in his bones.

Grace pulled up her knees again and brightened. "What about you, though? Long history of girls chasing you around the fire station?"

"Nah," he said. "I tend to get involved with the crazies, too. Because of that, I don't really *do* relationships. You know." He touched the *nicho* and turned. "How crazy are you nowadays, exactly?"

"I would have said not at all, not anymore." Grace looked at him, and their gazes tangled for one long moment. "But I'm not so sure now."

Tox felt something build inside him. A determination of sorts. But it was blended with heated excitement, a fine tremor that made his hands feel jittery. "I should go."

"I'm probably not crazy enough for you, though. I'm pretty sure about that," she said, standing. She came forward the two steps it took to reach him. "I'm hardly crazy at all."

"Hmmm." Tox lifted a hand and carefully, slowly, so as not to spook her, touched the strand of hair that kept falling over her eye. "Does it count if you're *driving* me crazy?"

"Maybe." She tilted her head to the side and rubbed her cheek against his hand. "You *should* probably leave. You're bad for me."

He could be so much worse for her, she had no idea. He ran the back of his fingers down the slope of her jaw, and let his thumb rest where it had wanted to all night, right on the plumpest part of her lower lip, exactly where he wanted to taste it again. "I'm good for you."

"Your nickname is Toxic."

"No truth in advertising," he said. "I even helped save your sister. Doesn't that make me good for something?"

Oh, shoot. Wrong words, wrong phrase. Her eyes widened, and he saw the incident flash in front of her again.

"Samantha ... How could I forget? Even for a minute?"

"What, that she's okay?" Tox trailed his finger down, over her chin, down her neck. Slowly. "She's fine."

"I could have lost her ... I can't—"

"Shhh, sweetheart." The endearment slipped out so easily. "She's sleeping. We're the only two people not sleeping in Darling Bay right now, I'd be willing to bet."

She lifted her chin so that his finger could find an even smoother trail down to the vee of her shirt. He paused at her neck, skimming it. A whisper of touch.

Then, instead of kissing her mouth, he leaned down and kissed there, in that sweet, warm spot, just under her chin. A soft kiss. A reassuring kiss.

But the noise she made in the back of her throat was anything but gentle. With a primal growl, she put her hands on both sides of his head, dragging his mouth up to hers. When they kissed, her tongue met his with a blaze that made him know he was lost.

He wrapped his arms around her, sliding his hands down so that he could cup her deliciously soft derriere. Then Grace shocked him. She lifted one leg, then the other, wrapping her strong thighs around his waist. He held her there, by her bottom. Climbing up him like that, she never even broke the kiss.

"Behind you," she said into his mouth.

He tried valiantly to take his lips away. "Wha ..."

"Don't stop," she pleaded, her hands pulling his head back to hers. "The bedroom's behind you. Go," she said.

He went.

CHAPTER 23

Grace woke in a happy tangle of legs and sunshine. It felt good.

She straightened her legs, pushing them against the wall, pressing her toes onto the cool lemon-colored paint.

It was the two extra-long legs that were wrapped with her own that she was concerned with. Heavy, muscular legs.

Screwing her eyes shut tightly, she tried to block out the ray of sun that lit up not only her own face, but Tox's. His chin was covered with what looked like a three-day beard growth. The hair on his bare chest ran downward, curving in at the sloping muscles of his stomach, headed under the sheet …

No, she had to focus on herself. Take inventory of her mental and physical states, just as she'd trained herself to do. From bottom to top. Calmly.

Her legs felt … weak. Still a little weak. It was a good thing he'd carried her into her bedroom.

The middle part of her body? Well, that had been a workout she hadn't expected. She was glad she'd been doing crunches. At least her core was strong enough. She grinned to herself at the thought.

Her heart? Oh, no, she couldn't think about that right now. She knew intuitively that she wouldn't be able to trust whatever she told herself. A guy like Tox? Last night had been ... No one had ever touched her like he had. He'd made her feel like a kitten and a sex doll and best of all, like she was someone he could never get enough of. No matter what she'd done, he'd wanted more. And she'd felt the same way about him. She'd wanted him harder and deeper, and then again. She blushed as she remembered the third "again" she'd wanted. And gotten.

And then, as dawn had broken as rosy as she'd known her cheeks must have been, he'd kissed her to sleep. Quite literally, she'd gone to sleep with his mouth on hers. Breathing each other in.

She'd never known such tenderness.

Yeah, so she just wouldn't think about her heart. Whatever.

Her head. That was the problem. Her brain. Tox wasn't good for her. She knew that. In the logical area of her thoughts, she knew that he shared nothing in common with her pursuit of health. He didn't sleep. He ate fast food, fried food, and way too much sugar. He drank too much coffee. He didn't take care of a simple injury, making it worse.

And worse, he couldn't cultivate relationships. Or, in his words, he didn't really *do* them. That meant he broke women's hearts. She wouldn't be one of them. No way.

Still, she felt her resolve slipping. Was it that he couldn't cultivate relationships with women? Or was it that he wouldn't? Was it something he could fix? With help, maybe?

She regretted the thought as soon as it flitted through

her mind. *This.* She flipped back the sheet only to realize that she, too, was naked as a jaybird. *This* was why she got into crappy relationships with men. Because she let them get away with it.

No more. She'd promised herself that. But she let her eyes crawl over Tox's sleeping body one more time, as she reached slowly for her robe hanging on the back of the bedroom door. Oh, his legs, so long under that sheet. His feet hung off the end of her bed. The perfect naked chest ... Those amazing sea-green eyes.

She gave a squeak as she realized his eyes were wide open, staring at her with amusement.

"Good morning, gorgeous," he drawled, pushing himself up on one elbow.

"Your hair is crazy!" The words were out before she could stop them. "I mean ..."

He ran his fingers through his mop of hair slowly. "I do have mad scientist hair in the morning. What are you doing up?"

"Coffee!" she exclaimed. "I like coffee."

As she ran out of the room, she could hear him laughing behind her.

———

SHE THOUGHT that maybe by the time she got it brewed and had poured them both cups he would have been dressed and ready to get on with his day. After all, she had to get to the clinic to post that she would be closed for the day and get to the hospital as soon as possible. She wanted to bring Samantha home and watch over her, fussing over how many blankets to pile on and making her take anti-inflammatories until she was strong enough to answer all the questions Grace had stored up for her.

Yeah. Maybe when she brought Tox coffee, he'd be dressed. Ready to head out.

No such luck. When Grace ventured back in the room that still smelled like warmth and sex—their sex—he was sitting up, leaning on her headboard as if he'd been born to do it, flipping through a Yoga Journal magazine.

He held it up. "You know about this kundalini stuff?"

"I've heard of it."

"Shoot." He let out a low whistle, which she thought was related to his thinking about the Svadhistana until she noticed his eyes weren't on the magazine anymore. Instead, he appeared intently focused on the way her yellow silk robe parted when she leaned to hand him his cup.

"So," she said briskly. "Do you have to work today?"

"Nope. I'm on my four-day."

Well, so much for that method of getting him out of her house. She *did* have to get him out, right? She couldn't let him stay. No. She couldn't. For a moment, though, she couldn't remember why not. The X-rated images that danced in her mind, both of what they did last night and what she still *wanted* to do to him, made her feel like she should just let the robe slip open a little more.

So she did. Really, it was an experiment. Grace was kind of required to see if what they'd had last night wasn't just a product of too much heightened fear and emotion after her sister's crash.

So she twisted as she reached for her cup, tugging the clip out of her hair at the same time. Her hair tumbled around her shoulders. When she turned to meet Tox's gaze, she made sure she twisted back a little too far. The silk of the robe was slippery. It never did stay together the way it was supposed to.

She bit her lower lip and then wet it with her tongue, never letting go of his gaze.

Something in his eyes—he reminded her of something ... an animal of some sort.

As he launched himself at her with a roar she realized what it was. He was a huge jungle cat, ready to take down its quarry.

And he took her down, hard. She was flat on her back on the bed, robe thrown to the floor, condom in his hand and then on, and he was in her, without preamble or discussion. And as he moved in her, so fast, so *hard*, and his eyes stayed on hers. Mine, his eyes said. Mine, mine, *mine*.

She knew her eyes said the same thing back to him.

She also knew she'd regret it later. She'd probably regret nothing more.

But now, for this moment, as her fingers dug deeply into his back, moving to match his thrusts, she was his, and he was hers, and nothing had ever felt so right. Ever.

CHAPTER 24

The next time Grace got out of bed, she was more determined. The hospital. That's where she had to be.

She showered, and by the time she got out, Tox was pulling on his shirt. "I gotta go see a man about a dog. Literally." He stood. "Walk of shame time, I guess."

She smiled. "At least you're not in heels."

He stuck out a leg and examined his boot. "What? I could pull that off."

Grace had no doubt he could. "I like a man in drag," she said. "It's hot."

Tox said, "I've seen some pretty men. I won't argue with you on that," and Grace felt herself fall a little further.

She put in her silver hoop earrings, the ones Samantha had given her years ago. At one point, she'd wondered if Sam had stolen them. Or bought them with money made in a way that could get a person jailed. Or worse.

She fingered them gingerly. She loved them, no matter where they came from.

"You look incredible."

Surprised, Grace looked down at herself. "Me?" Her voice felt high and nervous, as if she were speaking while crossing a tightrope. She was only wearing a black t-shirt and jeans with old yellow cowboy boots. Her favorite comfort outfit. "I thought I looked kind of ... not that good."

"One," he pulled her back into the wide circle of his arms, "You do look that good. And two, I wasn't looking at your clothes."

He kissed her, and Grace came perilously close to forgetting why she had her keys in her hands.

"No," she said, pulling away with difficulty, ignoring the heat that rose inside her. "I'm going."

"I want to see you later," Tox said.

"Okay ..." she said. The word was easy, but it fell into the space between them awkwardly. "I mean ... when Sam is better, and when you're on your time off again, you go in for a couple of days tomorrow, right? It's just ..."

"Grace." He tilted her head up by touching her chin. "We had a good time, right?"

*A good time.* Is that what people called it now? Was it that easy for him? "Yeah."

"Then maybe you'll think about giving me a call later today."

"Sure."

"Or come by the station tomorrow."

"Sure."

He nodded and released her. "Seems like that's the best I'm going to get out of you, then."

"You got the best out of me last night, I think." She wanted to sound bold and brazen, but instead, she just sounded shy.

He laughed.

Grace didn't like the confusion she felt inside. What

was wrong with her? She was scared to see any more of him, in case she really did fall, and at the same time, she hated the thought of *not* being around him.

They left the house together. It felt strange to turn and lock the door behind them. Like any other couple on a Wednesday morning. They walked down the steps, their arms brushing. With a salute at the edge of her walkway, Tox grinned as he turned right to head to his truck.

Walking toward her car, Grace wondered how in the world he could be so casual. Maybe he was that used to leaving the house of a woman in the morning? The thought made her feel faintly ill. But she would ignore it ...

Behind her came fast footfalls. A large hand at her elbow. Tox spun her, pulling her into his arms.

"You fit here, you know that?"

Grace's mouth dropped open.

"I love the way you fit in my arms. This could be good. It might actually be *good*," said Tox. Then he kissed her once, hard. "I just wanted to make sure I told you that."

He let her go. Grace watched him walk away, her fingers on her lips, trying to swallow the smile that just wouldn't go away.

## CHAPTER 25

In the hospital, Samantha said, "It's about time!"

Grace pulled out her cell phone and glanced at it. "You said you would call me, though. Oh."

"I've been calling since last night. They said I could go home at seven this morning, but you never came."

"I'm sorry," Grace said. "I didn't see the messages. I had my ringer off, I guess. I'm so sorry. How are you feeling?"

Sam stretched one arm in front of her and then the other. "I hurt. I feel muscles I didn't even know existed. Ever."

"You look amazing," said Grace, touching the side of her sister's face softly.

Samantha winced and pulled away. "I saw. I look like an alcoholic ex-prizefighter."

"Who got in a car wreck after losing his last round."

"After being hit on the head with a frying pan by his wife when she found out he was cheating on her," said Samantha.

"Something like that," Grace said.

Samantha made a buzzing noise and stood, slowly. "Not

what you tell the lady getting sprung. You tell her she's pretty."

"You're pretty."

Margarita, the head nurse poked her head in. "Yes, lovey, you're pretty."

It was true—even bruised and swollen, Samantha's delicate features inspired a take-care-of-me vibe that every person who popped in and out of the room seemed to feel. Each nurse smiled, touched her somewhere, wished her the best.

"That makes me feel better. That's what a girl needs to heal." Samantha said, tossing her hair. "Ow. Dang it. I can't do that right now."

"So don't do it. Come on. Let's blow this dump."

In the hospital corridor, Grace put her arm around her sister's shoulder. Samantha wrapped her arm around Grace's waist. Together, they went home.

---

GRACE GAVE HER SISTER AN HOUR.

Then she went in her room. "So."

Samantha sighed and flopped backward onto her pillow. "I hope you're here to bring me more tea."

She knew better than that. "Who is he?"

Sam raised her hands and let them flop onto her stomach. "Just a guy."

"What's his name?"

"Justin."

"What does he do?"

"Why does that always matter so much to you?"

Grace sat on the edge of the bed, conscious that if she said the wrong thing now she could erase the careful trust that had built between them over the last year. "It matters because it says a lot about a person."

"Fine. He doesn't have a job, as it happens."

*Drug dealer. Pimp. Gambler.* It didn't help that Grace had accidentally dated all those guys, too. "What does he want to do?"

"He's an environmentalist."

"Oh, yeah?"

Samantha sighed. "He has money from his parents. I guess, like, a lot of money."

That would explain the car at least.

"He does something with cleaning water."

"What?" Grace tried to keep the skepticism from her voice, but found it impossible. "So you're dating a mob boss."

"Jesus, Grace."

"A mob boss wannabe?"

"Why can't he just be a guy? A normal guy?"

"Where did you meet him?"

Her sister crossed her arms over her chest. "I don't have to tell you."

Awesome. Had Samantha fallen off the wagon again? Was she at the bar while Grace was at work? "How's your drinking doing?"

Samantha took in a loud breath. "You know what? You always ask me things like *that*. How's my drinking? How's my using? Why not ask the more accurate question. How's my sobriety going? Today?"

"Your defensiveness makes me worry that I'm going in the right direction."

Samantha stood, wincing as she did so. "I'm getting out of here."

"Where are you going?" Grace watched as Samantha shoved clothes into a duffel bag. "You can't just go."

Samantha didn't say anything. She just moved into the bathroom and began collecting her toiletries into a plastic case.

"Come on. Talk to me. I'm only concerned about your well-being."

Pausing, a bottle of eye-makeup remover in her hand, Samantha turned to face Grace. "I don't think you are."

Pain knifed through Grace. "Of course I am. I'm never anything *but* concerned about you."

"That's the whole problem. Your concern isn't flattering."

"But ..."

"I'm not a junkie."

"You—"

"I had a problem with drugs. I was an addict. But I'm not anymore. I'm clean. I'm sober. I'm healthy."

"But this guy—"

"Is none of your business, Grace."

It felt like a sucker punch. How many times had Grace heard this from her sister? How many times had Samantha said she was fine, only to call a month later from a bus stop in an inland state, needing fare money home? And then never arriving?

"You have to tell me at least something. What his last name is. Where he lives. Where you're *going*."

"I have a place to stay." Samantha threw an eyelash curler into the bag.

"With him? Isn't he still in the hospital?" Grace had tried to check on him in the hospital but the nurses hadn't let her go inside the ICU. No one but family.

"Gracie," Sam said in a soft voice. "You should call that guy."

"Who?" Grace tried to keep her face blank.

"Please. I know why you were late this morning to get me. It was obvious. Call Tox and have a good time."

"No. *You're* the most important thing in my life." It was true. It would always be true.

Samantha said, "But you have to let me make my own mistakes."

*Not when you've already made so many.* "Are you in love with him?" She followed Samantha through the living room and out to the porch.

"Of course I'm not. I just met the guy. But I know where his key is, and he'd already asked me to stay. I talked to him in the hospital and he said I could crash at his place."

Grace threw her hands in the air. "Why not? You already crashed with him once."

"Oh, *come* on, Grace."

"You can't do this. You're better than this."

"I know," said Samantha. "You did an amazing job of teaching me that, okay? But I can't handle you anymore."

"What do you mean?" Grace would agree to anything at all, if Samantha would just stay here, where she could keep an eye on her. Where she could check on her at night. Make sure she was fed. Safe. Healthy. "I'll back off. I know I can be pushy."

"Pushy?" Samantha dropped the bag at her feet and faced her, hands on her hips. "If I make hot chocolate at night, you get up to check whether I'm doing it right."

"The two-percent is just better for you."

"I like whole. Just like sometimes I stay up too late and I'm tired the next day. Sometimes I eat the whole pint of ice cream. *In one sitting.*"

Grace flinched.

"My body, my rules. How many times have you told me that? I get to make my own decisions, that no man can make them for me?"

"No man can," said Grace, reached out a hand. "Don't let him."

"I won't. And I'm not going to let you either. It's my life. Not yours. *Mine.* You know I love you, Grace, but you need to take care of yourself. And no one else."

Samantha went down the steps, turned right, and set off on foot down Taylor Street, toward the water. Grace sank with a thump to the top step of the porch.

It was a perfectly valid argument.

That was the hardest part. Her sister was right.

CHAPTER 26

Methyl was terrorizing Station One.

Even though Tox thought he hadn't let her out of his sight since he'd arrived to work that morning, she'd already managed to chew up Bonnie Maddern's right boot, Mazanti's A's baseball hat, and a full pack of paper plates, leaving nothing but slobber and rubble. Every time he blinked, every time he thought about waking with Grace yesterday morning, in her warm bed ... every unfocused moment was a moment Methyl ate something ill-advised.

Warm smells of garlic bread wafted from the kitchen where Knowland was fixing up his famous blue cheese spaghetti plates. On the big screen, the baseball game was only important to Hank.

"I thought you said she was sickly," said Bonnie, holding up her boot. "You gonna pay for this?"

"What? The station dog doesn't get a free pass or two?"

"The *station* dog?" Chief Barger came into the day room carrying a destroyed iPod charger. "When did we get one of those?"

Tox looked sideways at Bonnie who wasn't hiding her

laughter. "Just for A shift, when I'm here. And I have an extra one of those cords in my locker. I'll give it to you."

"You better. And you better check with HR about having a canine in the house."

Bonnie pulled the broken, wet lace out of her boot. "You realize that if he checks with HR he's dealing with my sister Lucy, right? And that she has twelve dogs and fourteen cats?"

Barger's spindly eyebrows shot straight up. "Darling Bay has a limit of four of each."

"Then sic June in Code Compliance on her, but seeing as they're tennis partners, I don't think you're going to get much traction there. Lucy's been trying to get us to adopt a station dog for two years. The only thing she'll say no to is us finding our own."

Methyl chose that moment to race into the day room, make one fast lap around the long table, and then sit comfortably on Chief Barger's foot.

"She likes you, Chief," said Tox. "I haven't seen her do that to anyone else." He hoped no one told the truth—that Methyl's favorite place seemed to be on anyone's shoe. Or under a table, chewing on a shoe.

Barger bent to scratch her head. "Well, heck. That's something, isn't it? Huh."

Methyl made a move as if to go to Tox, so he held up his hand. *Stay.*

Maybe the mutt knew what was good for her. She tilted up her head so that Barger could better reach her ears.

"Cute little thing. I suppose ..."

Tox waited, surprised to find he was holding his breath. He needed this dog to stay in the house with him when he was at work. Working a forty-eight, how would he keep

Methyl if he couldn't? And something about this dog just turned him inside out.

The dog and Grace. They softened him. He wasn't at all sure if that was a good thing. But it was something important, so much more important than he could have dreamed.

"Wait." Chief Barger locked eyes with Tox. "She's yours?"

"Yep."

Barger laughed. "The Angel of Death has a dog? How long you expect to keep *her* around?"

He would have told anyone else to shut up, but to Barger he just said, "Ah, quit it."

"No, I'm telling you. Look at this dog, Mazanti. Doesn't she look like she's about to fall over?"

Guy Mazanti squirmed in his recliner to look. "She looks fine to me, but Tox just better be careful with her. I wouldn't trust him with a dog. And don't get too close to her. She's gassy. Methyl's a perfect name."

Everyone laughed. Tox tried to laugh along with them, but it wasn't that funny. He didn't mean to be the guy in whose arms people died. He never asked for that role.

"Me and Methyl are gonna go play fetch in the south lot. And none of you are invited."

Good-humored laughter followed him through the bay and outside.

From the parking lot, the station had a partial view of downtown Darling Bay and a slice of the harbor. The sun was just setting, and when Tox got over his mild irritation at the ribbing of his coworkers, he realized he was enjoying the heck out of this—tossing the tennis ball he'd found with the sports equipment in the storage room, watching Methyl tumble toward it, tripping over her own golden legs. "You'll get it, girl. You'll catch on."

She was smart, that much was obvious. In the three and half days he'd had her, she'd already picked up—well, for a second there, he'd thought she was close to getting "sit." But he'd keep working with her. Even if she wasn't the brightest flare in the box, she was his. Every second that she wasn't chewing on something or sitting on people's feet, she was pressed against him, as if to remind him she was still there.

Dang it. Tox had fallen for two girls in the space of a week. He'd fallen hard. The image of Grace's coffee-colored eyes overshadowed the sunset in front of him, and he wondered what she was doing right now. Was she thinking about him? Moving in that little kitchen of hers, cooking something heart-healthy and organic? Soup, maybe, with the smells of oregano and thyme filling the air? Tox tossed the ball and Methyl chased it under the oleander bush with enthusiasm.

She hadn't called him yesterday. Then again, he hadn't called her. Tox had been trying to give her some space, and he'd made it clear the ball was in her court. He'd been surprised by how cut he'd felt last night when he'd been going to sleep. He'd wanted to see her. Wanted to kiss her again.

The truth was, Tox kind of felt like kissing her every night.

Doggone it, he would call her tomorrow, on the second day of his tour. Then maybe the next day they could have dinner at his place. No, hers. That way she'd feel comfortable and safe, surrounded by her own things. Home was important to her, he could tell. She needed to control her environment. He could understand that. Would she mind if he came up behind her in the kitchen and nuzzled her neck while she rinsed the knife before asking him to turn on the grill?

Tox shook his head, watching the dropping sun light the harbor a golden-edged pink. He was going soft in the head over a woman.

It felt good.

The tones went off, four of them in a row. Tox snapped his fingers. "Methyl. Come." He waited, clicking on her leash. If the engine was on the run for this call, he'd leave her here, tied to one of the concrete posts that protected the fuel pumps. He'd already placed a bowl of water and some kibble there, along with a thick wool blanket, in case a call came in. He hoped she didn't howl when she was left alone, but he didn't really have a choice.

Sue's voice, more grating than Lexie's, came over the loudspeaker, reading the call signs of the units assigned. When she listed "Engine One," Tox ran for the bay, Methyl already safely anchored.

The huge doors rolled up. Strobes flashed. In the kitchen, he knew, the stove and oven were shutting off, as the barbecue would be if they'd been using it tonight. All of it automated, so the station didn't burn down in the engine's absence.

Firefighters poured out of the day room, into the bay. It was a structure fire, and from Sue's report, it sounded like it might be good. "Multiple calls, smoke and flames showing from two windows." Behind her voice could be heard the phone, ringing off the hook.

"A lot of calls," shouted Coin as he swung up into the driver's seat. "Always a good sign."

"A good sign of a bad sign," said Tox, pulling on his turnouts and jumping into the rig.

Hank Coffee, always the slowest of the three, was shoving his arms into his jacket while he tried to jam on his second boot. He hauled himself into the back and slammed the door. "I'm in!"

"I was leaving without you if you weren't," said Coin.

As he hit the lights and sirens and updated dispatch they were en route, Tox felt the same thing he always did on the way to a fire: unadulterated excitement mixed with the tiniest touch of fear. It was heady, like clear-burning alcohol, and he was an addict. He had the best job in the whole wide world.

CHAPTER 27

Grace was finishing a solo dinner—a baked fillet of cod with too much basmati rice because she had no idea how to cook rice for one—when her phone made a foreign beep.

It was the fire app Samantha had installed on her phone yesterday, before they'd fought. "So you can hear if your guy goes somewhere," Samantha had said, showing her how to turn it on.

"He's not my guy."

Samantha had shrugged good-naturedly. "Then just to keep you apprised of what goes on in your town."

The phone kept beeping. "*Structure Fire*," read the pop-up box on her phone. She hit the open button, and suddenly her phone was making noise, voices saying words she didn't really understand. The map showed that it wasn't far away. A couple of blocks. Come to think of it, she'd thought she'd smelled something burning in her oven when she was cooking the fish but now that she stuck her nose out the kitchen door, she could smell smoke on the wind.

Tox's voice, startling and clear, cut through all the

chatter on the live radio dispatch. "Engine One," he said. "On scene. Two-story residential house, flames showing on the bravo and charlie side. Citizen reports explosion. Possibly hazmat, cook house. Incoming units, use precaution. Next due, charge the LDH. Engine One has Miranda Command."

Grace felt a mixture of fear and unwarranted pride. He sounded so ... in charge. Competent. Like he was going to blow out the fire himself, with his own breath.

A dispatcher who wasn't Lexie—maybe Sue?—responded, her voice electric with intensity. "Command, be advised, reports of two people inside. Repeating, possible two people trapped, last seen in the second floor hallway, one male adult, one female juvenile. Command copy?"

Tox was terse but clear. "Copy. Engine Two on scene, passing command. We'll be rapid intervention crew, making entrance."

"Copy, Engine One RIC."

Grace didn't know what all the words meant, but she knew one thing—it didn't sound good. She was pulling on her running sneakers before she knew what she was doing. It wasn't until she'd laced them and her hand was on her front door that she realized she was being ridiculous. She couldn't go to a *fire*. How could she have even thought of doing that? What would Tox say, if he looked out from doing his job to find her in the certainly inevitable crowd of lookie-loos?

She would help nothing. She *could* help nothing.

It was a terrible thought. No wonder people wanted to be firefighters and doctors and nurses. Helping was altogether a better, easier choice than choosing to do nothing. She walked back into the kitchen and started the kettle for tea.

Grace sat at the kitchen table, pushing away the plate of half-eaten fish and rice. In one hand, she held her phone, staring at the house on the map where the fire units were. She listened to Tox say something about a second alarm, his voice tight with stress but still easy to understand. In the other hand, she gripped her mug of tea. It cooled as she forgot to drink it.

The squawks from her phone bled into each other. Grace heard beeps and then Sue recited a list of more engines and trucks.

"I need medics on the bravo side," said a man's voice. Not Tox's. "We've got three victims. One firefighter down."

Grace felt a chill run through her. She might not know anything about firefighting, and it was only a guess, but her intuition knew who would have been taking the risks inside that house. She knew which firefighter was down.

And there was nothing she could do but put her head down on the table, her arm still outstretched holding her phone, as if it were something that could save him.

## CHAPTER 28

When Tox opened his eyes, he saw yellow. A lot of yellow. Yellow helmets, yellow turnouts, even Coin's vaguely yellow, sick-looking face.

There was an oxygen mask on his face. He yanked it down to his chin. "What the ..." He tried to sit up and gasped with pain.

"Oh, no, brother." A firm hand—Hank's—pushed him back down.

He looked around. They were moving, and he was in pain. That's all his smoke-addled brain could figure out at first.

Behind Hank's head he saw a medical cabinet as familiar to him as his own first-aid box at home. Okay, he was in the back of the rescue ambulance. And wow, he hurt.

"What happened?" It was painful to talk, too. Smoke inhalation, obviously. He did an inventory of his body—not burned. Unless they already had the morphine in him. But no, if he had the good stuff on board, he wouldn't have felt his back like he did. And holy cow, he felt it.

"You don't remember?"

Tox thought as hard as he could. They shouldn't have gone in, he remembered that. It was a meth house, a cook gone bad. Tox, as the hazmat expert, should have insisted no one entered. But there were people inside. "Inside. Upstairs. A man. Big guy." The shape came back to him, a man's body in the darkened, smoke-filled hallway.

The smaller shape lying next to him.

Hank nodded and kept his eyes on Tox's vitals. "Yeah, the owner of the house. Mazanti got him out."

"And the girl?" Now he remembered. In the smoke, he'd given the sign to Mazanti to drag out the man—he'd carry the female. It had probably been a boil-over, and he knew the solvents and gases inside were probably unstable.

The little girl. She'd been so light in his arms.

"They're working her," said Hank simply.

Tox knew Hank meant they were giving her CPR. "Who?"

"Rescue Three."

Tox coughed, and a sharp, knife-like pain lanced his spine. "Whose shift is it?"

"Knight, Sims, and Berkley."

"Catch up to them. You have to be on board. I wouldn't let Sims do CPR on a horse."

Hank shook his head and tried to replace the oxygen mask. "Sims is good. She'll be fine."

It was Hank's lying face. "How many times in our career have I heard you tell someone that?"

"Lots." Hank paused. He didn't look at Tox. "Sometimes it's true."

"Not when you say it like that."

"Come on, buddy. Leave it, will you? What's your pain level right now?"

"Now? It's about a hundred out of ten."

Hank stretched to grab the bag that held the morphine. "You're getting eight."

"It's just my back." And his lungs. And his ribs. "Make it four and I'll take it. Did I fall?"

"Like a stack of lumber."

*Crap.* "Did I fall on *her*?"

Hank smiled. "No way. You carried her out like she was your own daughter. Handed her to Sims—"

"Why would I do *that*?"

"—because you were about to pass out and he was the closest to you. You went down and smacked your head on the pavement. Your helmet got the brunt of it, but I think that's how you hurt your back, the recoil when you bounced back up."

"Gotta love a leather helmet." Some of the new guys liked the composite New York style but give Tox his old leather one for head and smack protection any day. "I hate morphine," Tox said through gritted teeth. Bright white spots danced at the edge of his vision. Man, this pain *sucked*. "How's the fire?" Tox hadn't ever left a fire still burning.

"They have knock down. Here comes your fix." Hank fixed the needle and prepped it to go in his line.

"I'm telling you. Only a little. I hate the way it feels. I want to see the little girl at the hospital. I want to be okay for it."

"Tox," snapped the normally mellow Hank. "Shut up."

Hank usually had the longest fuse on their crew. Tox hadn't seen him like this in years. "She's not okay, is she?"

Hank looked out the small side window, as if to judge how far they were from the hospital. Like Tox was going to get seen anytime soon, with an incoming code blue kid. "Nah. She's not."

There wasn't anything to say to that. Tox should have carried out the man. Given the girl to Mazanti to carry. The Angel of Death had struck again.

He closed his eyes and let the morphine's dull hum sink into his bones. It did nothing for his soul.

## CHAPTER 29

Grace paced past the fire station again. Eight times she'd done it now, hoping that she'd just "happen" to be passing by when they pulled back in. She'd heard on the phone app when they started releasing units, letting them go back to their home stations. She hadn't heard Engine One being released yet, but it was possible she'd missed it. She didn't understand all of the radio traffic.

No one had come back yet, not the truck that lived at Station One, nor the red SUV she assumed belonged to a chief or something. It was just her and the other people out for their evening strolls, only they just went past the station once. Not like her.

A blue curtain twitched at the yellow house across the street, and Grace wondered if the neighbors were getting suspicious of her. Well, who cared? What would they do? Call in a suspicious-looking exercising woman who was obsessed with the firehouse?

She checked her phone again. She hadn't dared call Tox —of course not—but she'd texted him, hoping he'd text back, assuring her that he wasn't the "firefighter down" she'd heard. But she'd heard nothing back. She'd texted Lexie, too, in the hopes that she was working tonight, but had only heard silence from her, too.

Grace paused at the end of the long driveway that curved around to the back of the station. A strange howl floated on the wind. A dog's complaint.

A dog who sounded like Methyl.

Sure enough, the little blond puppy was tied to a concrete post. She started wriggling as soon as she saw Grace, her back end jumping with excitement. "Okay! Here I am! Here I am." She unsnapped the leash from where it had been secured to itself, and Methyl didn't give her a second's chance. She leaped up into Grace's arms, scrabbling until she had her front paws on Grace's right shoulder.

Grace held the dog like a big, furry baby. "You've put on a bit of weight already, huh?" The relief was palpable. Here was Tox's dog. Tox had to be okay, because he had a dog now. Even though the logic wasn't sound, Grace clung to it, unable to think about the alternative.

Lexie's orange Mini pulled into a back parking stall. She jumped out. "I was down the coast. I headed back as soon as I heard the call go out—I know Sue and Wendy probably need help in there. Wanna come in?"

"Yes," said Grace. She did. Desperately.

"That your dog?"

"It's Tox's."

Lexie's face registered her surprise. "Wow. I'm off a day and the whole world turns inside out."

"Tell me about it."

# CHAPTER 30

Tox was put in his own room at the hospital, something the tiny Darling Bay ER rarely did. He knew it was done to keep him out of the mix, but he resented it. Hard.

Unfortunately, he was strapped to the bed with not one but two IVs, and while he knew he could extricate himself from under the tubes and wires, he was too exhausted to do so. Yet. Just give him a few minutes, and Tox knew he'd be right up and fighting again.

Chief Barger gave a short knock at his door and then entered. "How are you doing, champ?"

The chief was only nice like that when he had an unpleasant task to do.

"She didn't make it, huh?" Tox looked straight at the chief, keeping an eye on the mustache. A lot could be told from Chief Barger's mustache.

"She's still alive." The mustache wobbled.

"Great. That means she won't be soon."

Barger shook his head. "I'm so sorry to tell you this, Clement."

Ouch. His first name. No one but HR used his first name. And the Chief.

"But they're going to harvest her organs tonight. Her parents have decided."

Harvest. As if she was some kind of field. As if that somehow made it okay. It didn't. A child should never have to give up a life to save another child. Never.

Tox rubbed his eyes, not caring how the IVs dug into the back of his hand. He was on so much pain medication he could barely feel it anyway. "Wait," he said. "Her parents?"

Barger said, "Yeah. That's the good thing. Mazanti got Dad out and they got pulses on the way to the hospital. Mom was at work, she's here now with him."

"Cause determined?"

"Meth lab.." Barger's voice was big, as if the louder he talked the quicker he could move through the moment and get out of Tox's room.

Fine by Tox.

No matter what, that father had to wish he'd never woken up. That's why it didn't matter. Nothing mattered. A man in Darling Bay this morning had a kid. Now he didn't.

Tox wanted to be alone so he could practice steeling his expression. "I'll be fine, Chief." What a load of crap. "I just need to get back to work and I'll be fine."

The mustache jumped this time, and even through his morphine haze, Tox knew that was serious.

"Look, Clement. You're gonna be out a while."

"It's my back. That's all. I put it out coming down. My neck's been hurting, it's all connected, you know ... I was running fast so I hit the ground the same way." Tox wished he could remember running down the stairs with the little girl, but he couldn't. He *really* wished he could remember handing her over to Sims, but that was gone, too. "I'll take a week off and be back the next tour."

"It's not going to be that easy, son."

"Oh, yeah. It is." Insubordination didn't count in a hospital, right?

"You've had, what, nine deaths in the last twelve months?"

"Maybe."

"You know Darling Bay has only had thirteen all year. You've been on three-quarters of them."

"I work a lot of OT. So?"

"So that means time off."

"Says *who*?"

The mustache firmed into a straight line. "Says me. Take the mandated time. And you don't come back till you're medically cleared."

"I will be."

"And by medically," Barger tapped his forehead. "I mean up here."

"A shrink."

"It's not the end of the world."

Tox stuck out his chest, a frustrating thing to try to do while lying almost flat in a hospital bed. "I'll get cleared in one visit."

"Good for you, then. We want you back, son. But we want you back with a sound back and a clear mind."

Tox chewed the inside of his lip. The thing he wanted to ask he couldn't take back.

"What?" Barger was itching to get out of the room, Tox could tell. He was almost out. He couldn't blame him.

"Would anyone have lost her, you think?"

Barger's eyes softened and his mustache drooped. "I wasn't going to tell you."

"What?"

"But it'll come up in the after-action report ... You don't remember?"

Tox's heart quickened. "I don't remember anything after picking her up."

"You went the wrong way. You went into a closet with her. Dropped her. Mazanti had to leave the guy, go get you, turn you around and give you back the little girl."

Tox saw a veil of black dancing at the edge of his vision. "It was my fault."

"We'll never know, Tox. She was probably too far gone, even then."

It wasn't true. That's what they told each other when something went wrong. *You can't fix dead.*

Only sometimes they could, and that was his *job*, to fix dead when he could. Especially when a little girl's life hung in the balance.

"I'm so sorry," said Barger.

As if words could do anything to dull the roar Tox heard in his head.

A nurse entered briskly, her scrubs covered with tiny rainbows. "How's your pain?" she asked.

"Too high."

The nurse nodded and filled a needle. Barger nodded sympathetically and left.

Tox closed his eyes and felt the morphine blaze up his back and then drag him under. He wished he could shut out the world for a lot longer than the medicine was going to help him do. Forever, maybe. So he could apologize to the girl. He didn't even know her name.

Right before he slept, a nurse touched him on the hand. "There's someone here who says she wants to see you."

*Grace*, Tox thought groggily. "No."

"Are you sure? She's got flowers and a real worried look."

"Sure. No. Send her away."

He didn't deserve her.

CHAPTER 31

It hurt.

Grace couldn't deny that it hurt a lot. Tox didn't want to see her.

At all.

She'd gone back to the hospital three times, once with flowers, once with a dumb little teddy bear, and once she'd sweet-talked the nurse into letting Methyl in inside a crate.

And every time, he'd said no. She couldn't come in.

At the clinic, she worked with her patients like normal, but Mrs. Little asked why she was so sad and if acupuncture would help her, too. "It probably would," Grace said. "I should find a practitioner, I guess."

From the other side of the room, Steve Swanson hooted. "You should find a boyfriend, that's what I think."

Mrs. Little shushed him, and Grace laughed lightly, but the embarrassment cut deep. It cut even deeper still when Mrs. Little said sotto voce, "I heard about you and that fire-fighter. None of them are any good, dear. My husband was a police officer. I know about firefighters."

"Oh," was all Grace could think to say as she checked a point on Mrs. Little's hand.

"Lazy," she whispered. "Just want to sit in their recliners all day. They don't really want to help. Ninety percent of the time there's a medical emergency, it's the cops who get there first and fix it, you know."

"Ah."

"You don't believe me. But you'll see." Mrs. Little nodded with authority. "You'll probably keep seeing him, because that's what young girls do. They like to do what's not good for them, but ..."

"That's not true," interrupted Grace. She couldn't help it. "I'm not young, I'm thirty-three. And I always do what's good for me."

"Then why do your eyes look so sad, dear?"

An hour later, as Grace locked the front door after the last patient, she asked herself the same question. Why was she so devastated by the rejection of a guy she'd gone out with once? She'd slept with him, yeah. Was that the problem? Grace didn't think so—she didn't place overmuch weight on worrying whether a sexual action was right or wrong. It just was. Sex was sex. Bodies were bodies. She knew how to treat them, how to make them feel good.

Sure, she thought, as she fell into the rocking chair on the glassed-in porch. Sex was good. Positive. It benefited the body, mind, and soul. Any connection with another human being was a good thing.

It was just that she'd had *such* a connection with him. Foolishly, she'd deluded herself into thinking it could be more.

That, combined with the fact that she had no idea where Samantha was ... Grace felt helpless.

She pulled out her phone and stared at the face of it as

she had approximately one million times this week. No text from Sam. Nothing from Tox.

Nothing at all.

Grace wasn't usually scared to death of the big things. She'd nursed her mother until she died, not minding washing her, taking care of the body that had brought her into the world as her mother left the same. She'd taken care of her sister over and over again, never sure it was going to work, never confident Samantha would straighten out, would really drop the drugs, leave the men, never sure if she'd really mean it when she said she was starting over. And Grace had opened this practice by herself, with money she'd saved by working her butt off for other people, ordering water and salads when she went out to eat with friends, knowing every penny saved was another penny toward her dream. She wasn't scared to go after what she wanted. Usually.

But sending these texts?

She was terrified.

The first one was to Samantha. "I'm sorry. I love you. I support you. I believe in you."

She sat, rocking nervously, the phone clutched tightly in her hand. She waited for the telltale conversation dots that would tell her her sister was typing back.

Nothing.

Her heart curled into a tiny ball inside her.

Grace took a deep breath and pushed her shoulders back, just like she told her patients to do. All right. On to the next, then.

The second text was to Lexie. "I need Tox's home address." He'd listed the station's address on the intake form he'd filled out at the practice.

The response was almost instantaneous. "No way."

"Yes way."

"He would never forgive me," Lexie texted back. "I have to work with the guy. He's a beast when he's grumpy."

"I don't care." Grace punched the send button with extra emphasis.

"No."

"I have to return his dog."

"Ow. 180 Canfield. Don't tell him it was me or I'm never splitting a sundae with you at Skip's ever again."

"Liar. How's next Thursday?"

"I'm in."

Grace's cell went dark. Quiet. She closed her eyes and hoped.

CHAPTER 32

Tox had been ignoring everyone who came to his door for the last three days. He hadn't even looked out the blinds. He knew—could tell by their knocks—who'd come by.

Coin's knock was polite but determined. He had stayed on the porch, knocking in a steady rhythm, for ten minutes.

Barger's knock was demanding. Easy to tune out. Tox had just turned up whatever inane TV show—something about cooking squid—was on until he went away.

Lexie had the food knock, and she left the tuna-fish casserole (the only thing she said she could cook) on his doorstep. He'd eaten it out of the glass dish with a plastic spoon.

He was waiting for Grace's knock. She had Methyl, after all. Lexie had texted him with the information when he was still in the hospital, and he'd felt a high level of relief —the dog was okay—with a similar level of resentment. Grace couldn't just have his dog. Methyl was supposed to be with him. He missed the feeling of her floppy, silken ears. He missed the soft panting she did when she sat on the couch next to him.

He also missed the way Grace smiled at him, like he was something special. Something to be watched, enjoyed.

So he stayed on his couch, waiting. He didn't know what he'd do if she came by.

When he finally heard her cheerful knock, though, Tox knew. He lifted his head once from the couch, looked at her shadow on the blinds, and lowered his head again. He wouldn't even stand up. Because if he moved, he'd open the door, and then he'd let her in, and that would be just about the worst thing he could do. He didn't trust himself, not an inch.

Holding his breath, he waited for her to knock again.

She didn't. Her shadow disappeared.

The disappointment was thick in his throat, unexpected and chilling. She sure hadn't tried very hard. He'd thought maybe ... but no. She was probably just trying to get his dog back to him. He'd get Lexie to pick Methyl up. Tomorrow, maybe. He couldn't do it today.

Tox stretched, pulling up the blanket so it came to his chin again. It was almost time for another pill, and even though he didn't want to take it, he knew he probably would. Just to escape this awful darkness for a couple of hours.

Then he heard a noise in the back yard. It wasn't loud— just a soft thud followed by a louder click. Exactly as if someone had climbed the fence.

## CHAPTER 33

G race had never broken into anything more than song and she expected to hear sirens at any moment. How fast did the cops come when a burglar alarm went off?

But the fence, really. It was chump change. She'd scaled it in seconds, her heart juddering in her chest. She was short of breath from the fear she felt, not from the physical exertion it caused. She landed on the balls of her feet and stood, ready to run.

Grace heard nothing. She opened the fence and led Methyl into the back yard, holding her leash tightly.

This was really pretty stupid. If Tox didn't want to answer the door, he didn't have to. Cripes knew, he had a good reason to avoid talking to anyone. His job had gone as wrong as any job could go—losing a *child*—and he was probably drunk and passed out on the floor, like any other reasonable person.

Then again, drinking on the meds he was surely on wouldn't be a good idea. Grace reached a slow hand out to the back doorknob and thought about the way alcohol metabolized when combined with prescription pain medication.

It was why she'd jumped the fence.

Someone had to check on him.

As she turned the knob, she hoped two things: that he wasn't dead, and if he was alive and awake, that he didn't have a gun.

The door opened with a slow creak. She closed her eyes and contorted her lips into a grimace, but it didn't quiet the door. Crap.

She stepped into a kitchen that looked as if it were normally neat and tidy. There was a place for everything, heavy-looking copper-bottomed pots hanging over the industrial stove, knives gleaming in a dark wood block. But the sink was full of dishes, and on second glance, she noticed that it was mainly glasses and cups, as if he'd been living on liquid.

Poor guy.

She heard something to the right, a scuffle. She should call out—she knew she should. But what if he was asleep and she scared him to death? That wouldn't be fair.

Grace skated across the floor in her tennis shoes, as quiet as she could make herself. She barely breathed. As if Methyl knew what they were doing, the puppy stuck close to her right foot, moving silently.

The open door led to a living room.

Across the room, next to the large plate glass window, was a couch.

On the couch with a blanket pulled up to his chin, Tox slept.

It wasn't fair, really, how handsome he looked while at the same time retaining such vulnerability. She sneaked closer, moving on tiptoe.

A foot away from him, Grace felt lightheaded, and she wasn't sure if it was because she was so close to him or because she'd forgotten to breathe.

His chest moved, and something inside her released, something she didn't even know she'd been holding on to. His breath was slow, even.

He was sound asleep.

Indulging in a brief fantasy, Grace let herself imagine lying down next to him, tucking herself along the length of his body. She would press her nose up, into the space there, just under his jaw, where it would be prickly and warm. In his sleep, he would roll to her, murmuring something she couldn't understand. And then, if she was lucky, she'd feel him becoming aroused ... He would get hard against her, and she'd tuck her hips, angling them against him and his arms would come around her, and he'd take a kiss from her, a kiss she'd be eager to give ...

No. Grace had to stop thinking like this. She could feel her heart rate speeding up, and she felt a thin trickle of sweat between her breasts. Plus, it was all she could do to prevent Methyl from jumping up on Tox. She had to stay bent over, one hand at the dog's collar, and Methyl still pulled. Grace did, though, understand the motivation to jump on that guy. She sure did. "C'mon, girl," she whispered. "We'll let him rest."

In the kitchen, she talked Methyl into lying on the dog bed, new and clean and plush. "He got you a pink sparkly dog bed? Wow, dog, someone must love you." That word—*love*—felt heavy and warm on her lips.

A sandwich first. It would be on the counter, ready to put in his hand when his eyes opened. Her theory that every single man owned the makings of a sandwich proved true. She made a thick ham and cheese, piling on the mustard, mayo and pickles. No one didn't love pickles. She found chips that weren't too stale and tucked them into the sandwich, too, pressing down on top to crush them in.

And heck. It looked so good Grace made herself one, too. She sat at the small kitchen table and chewed quietly, slipping bits of bread down to Methyl. It was an awful precedent to set, feeding the dog people food at the table. But that little blond face ... How could she resist?

When Grace was done eating her sandwich, making sure Tox's was safely at the back of the counter, away from where Methyl could possibly reach it, she did the dishes. Not just the ones she'd used, but all of them. She filled the sink with piping hot water and bubbles, enjoying the feel of the dishes coming out clean.

As Grace was drying them with a clean red tea towel she found in a drawer, she started. Oh, not this. She was acting like ... a wife. There was really nothing Grace disliked more than a woman who felt it was her duty to clean up after her man, unless it was a man who thought the same thing. In every relationship, no matter how short or unhealthy in other ways it had been, Grace had always made sure that chores were divided evenly, not by gender.

Here she was, Tox's spoons slipping through her fingers, clean, into the cutlery drawer. And she liked it.

Well.

Grace stood up straighter. She could fix this problem. The back screen door, when she'd let herself in, had squealed like a startled pig. She had been surprised the noise hadn't woken him, but he must still be exhausted, to say nothing of whatever meds he was or wasn't on. While Methyl snored in the kitchen, Grace explored the small attached garage until she found a bottle of oil and a screwdriver. It took her less than fifteen minutes to remove the rusty screws, oil the heck out of the hinges and replace the screen door. Satisfied, she moved it back and forth, back and forth, happy with its silence.

Next, she'd start organizing the tool shelf in the garage. She didn't have a clue how he could find anything in there when he needed it. She shut the kitchen's screen door once more with a good, solid click, and turned, the screwdriver and oil in her hands.

Tox stood there, barefoot on the tile. He held Methyl in his arms, and both of them looked shaggy.

His face was a thundercloud. "What are you doing to my *house?*"

## CHAPTER 34

It had been so hard, lying there completely still as she watched him. Did she think she'd been quiet? Breaking and entering with a *dog*? Methyl had wuffled and scraped her way along the hardwood floor, and Grace's half-whispers for her to be quiet had been hard not to react to. After she'd finished staring at him, he had let her work in the kitchen for a while. He'd been trying to figure out what to do. He'd wanted to rush to her, wrap his arms around her and refuse to let go. He also wanted to throw her out.

Then it had been kind of nice, listening to her putter around in the kitchen. It sounded like she was fixing something to eat, and while he'd kept his breathing slow and steady, he'd strained his ears to hear exactly where she was in the house. After she finished eating (and from the sound of it, feeding his dog something crunchy, too), and doing his dishes, she'd fixed his screen door.

That, it turned out, was way too much for him to ignore.

Grace's eyes went huge, and she dropped the screwdriver. "You're awake!"

"What did you do to my door?" Methyl scrabbled in his arms, and he set her on the floor.

She ignored him, turning and grabbing a plate from the kitchen counter. "I made you a sandwich."

"You what?"

Moving too fast, Grace thrust the plate forward and half the sandwich flew off and onto the floor, where Methyl inhaled it as her due within seconds.

"Are you serious?"

"*Dang* it," she said with feeling. "It's a *good* sandwich. I put chips inside. At least eat the other half."

"Chips. Inside."

She smiled, and Tox felt his heart twist in exactly the way it shouldn't. "It makes it crunchy and salty. It's delicious, even though I'll admit it's not very good for you. Please eat it." She paused and then held out the plate again, slower this time. "And please don't be mad I broke in."

He sighed and sat at the table. "You know, I liked that door squeaky."

"No, you didn't. No one could like that."

"I did."

"Why?"

Tox looked at her hard. "It alerted me when women broke into my house."

"But you didn't wake up—oh. You did."

He nodded slowly.

Grace put the plate in front of him. "You wanted to see what I'd do."

None of this was fair to her. "You should go."

"After you eat," she said, her voice resolutely chipper. She pulled out the opposite chair and dropped into it. She put both elbows on the table and leaned forward. "I'm not going anywhere till then."

"Anyone ever tell you you're a pain in the butt?"

"It's been mentioned. Please eat, Tox."

It wouldn't do any good. He knew that. Eating was temporary. It satisfied something that came and *went*. Hunger was like anything else—transitory. Fleeting. Like the pull he felt to her. No matter how strong it was, it didn't mean anything in the long run.

Why try to sustain anything? At all? When no matter what, everything ended?

He chewed, and while he could admit the chips were a good addition, he couldn't enjoy it. He couldn't enjoy anything, he thought. Maybe ever again.

"I'm sorry about what happened," said Grace. It sounded as if she meant it, as if she really were sorry.

But that didn't mean anything, either. "Nothing to do about it now."

"Sounds like there wasn't anything to do about it then, either."

He stared. If only her lips weren't so perfectly shaped, a soft cupid's bow, maybe then he could get them off his mind. "Yeah, there was. And besides, how would you know anything about it at all?" He knew he sounded rude. That was fine. That was what he was going for, after all.

"I talked to Lexie."

"Lexie wasn't there."

"She went in to dispatch that night."

"She wasn't on scene. She doesn't know a thing."

"She knows you did your best."

He grimaced. "That's what everyone always says to losers."

"Tox—"

"No, I'm right about this. Everyone is being so *nice*. I

wish they didn't feel like they had to be. Just for once, it would be a relief if someone called me on my bull."

"Really? You want me to ask how on earth you could let a child die from a fire you didn't start, weren't responsible for?"

Even her words hurt. "Yeah. How could I do that?"

"*Did* you do the best you could?"

"I'm pretty sure I did. It was a hazmat situation. We shouldn't have even gone inside, once we knew it was a lab. We weren't suited up, we didn't have the right respirators. But we did go in."

"Because you knew about the people who were trapped."

"And it wasn't enough."

"For the man, it was."

Tox bit back a curse. "He has to live his life without his daughter."

"But you guys saved *his* life."

"Great. So he'll go to jail for the lab. He could have killed dozens. Do you have any idea how volatile those chemicals are? The solvents alone put every responder in danger of contamination. We saved a criminal."

"How about last week, when you saved that baby in front of the fire station?"

He shook his head and pushed away the plate. "Totally different situation. That baby would have been fine no matter what I did. He was just postictal."

"All kids turn blue like that?"

"Yeah, after a seizure, they do."

"So nothing you did helped?"

"Probably not."

She kept prodding, blast her. "So you're saying you don't really help anyone at all in your job."

"Not usually." It was *true*. What they did—pick-up and put-backs, lift assists, rides to the hospital—unless they were hooked up to the shock box or the autopulse, they probably weren't helping that much. And in that case, those were machines doing the job of CPR now, not even the firefighters themselves most times.

"So whatever was going to happen to the little girl in the fire, you couldn't really help that, either? And from what you're saying, no one else could, either."

Tox didn't like where this was going. "I fell, did they tell you that? I fell, and took her with me. If I hadn't fallen the wrong way, pushing any good air she had left in her body right out her, if I hadn't made her inhale the superheated toxic fumes around us, she might have lived."

"That sounds like a terrible accident on top of a tragedy."

He exhaled heavily. Didn't she get it? "It's what I did that counts, not what I intended to do. That's all. I failed."

"That's not fair," she said, shaking her head. "What you intend to do counts a lot."

Tox waved his hand around the kitchen. "Is that kind of like what you've done here?"

"What?"

"You intended to fix my place up? So what, so you could move in or something?"

Grace gasped. "What?"

"You come in and make me food. Fatten me up. Trying to make me healthy."

She crossed her arms over her chest. "When was the last good meal you ate?"

"It's none of your business, actually."

"It is," she said, but her voice was softer now. "Besides, I added chips. Those aren't healthy."

"So I shouldn't have them in my house?"

"No, I'm not saying that, Tox." She closed her eyes as if trying to find something inside herself. "But I do believe that people should help each other."

"But you're not helping. That's your problem. You think you know better than anyone else. And you know what that translates into?"

"What?" She barely met his eyes.

"You come off as a know-it-all. Bossy as a new fire captain. You realize since you've known me you've advised me to change my diet, my form of exercise, my hair, and my house? That's not okay."

"I haven't—" but she broke off. It was true, and it was hitting her that he was right, he could see it on her face. Her expression crumpled.

He felt guilty, but whatever. Tox always felt guilty nowadays. "You even did my dishes. Who asked you to do that?"

"No one," she said defensively. "I was just trying to help. Just like I do with my sister, and now she won't talk to me, either. But I'm only ever trying to help."

"Who asked you to help, Grace?"

She picked up the red salt shaker and put it back down with a crack. "Who asked *you* to save the world?"

"No." Tox wouldn't let her turn this around on him. He was in the right here. "You don't get to go there."

"I don't? You have all this guilt about losing the girl, right?"

"Yeah. I do." With all the reason in the world.

"If Hank had lost her, would you be mad at him?"

It was a stupid thing to say. "You don't get it."

"I don't? I think that if it had been anyone else, you

would forgive them for being human. But you can't do that for yourself."

Tox thumped his open hand on the table, making both it and Grace jump. "There you go again trying to fix me!"

"So?" She didn't deny it, just kept looking at him with those big eyes.

"So you don't get to just fix whatever you want. That's probably why your sister's so mad at you. You and this God complex you have."

She gaped at him even more than she had been. "You're accusing me of having a God complex when you're the one who thinks you can save everyone from their fate?"

"Fate? You think that's why that girl was put on this earth? To die painfully in a fire?"

Grace's cheeks paled. "Was she in pain?"

*Probably*. But she didn't need to know that. "No," he lied. "She wasn't. But Grace, we have the same problem. We're both delusional. Neither of us are good for anyone else, no matter what we hope for on a good day." For one brief second, he wished he could take it back, to wipe that shocked and hurt look off her face, but it was too late.

She stood and brushed off the front of her shirt where it had gotten damp, probably while she was doing his dishes. "I guess I got this—us—wrong, then."

He wished she hadn't. He wished so hard she hadn't gotten a single thing wrong. But she had. "You can't fix me, Grace. You can't fix anyone, no matter how many needles you stick in them, no matter what tea you make them drink. Just back off. Of everyone."

Grace's mouth opened and then closed. Her eyes had lost that excited light, the light that came so naturally to her. He'd put that out. This was on him.

"I'm sorry," she finally said.

"Take the dog with you."

"No!" She pressed her lips together for a moment, and her chin quivered. "You need her. She needs you."

"Whatever. I don't care. About either of you." It was the worst thing he could think of to say. The one thing that would drive her out of his house. For good. He had to let her go now before he broke her even worse. It was too late for him. His body had betrayed him and even if he managed to fix his neck and back, now he had to pass a psych test before he could go back to work on the line. That would never happen. He knew he was too broken.

Tox was as good as his name, not good for anyone. Grace needed a real man.

A good man.

## CHAPTER 35

Grace wanted to be alone, but she didn't want to be at home. And she certainly didn't want to be at the clinic.

The beach, then. It was the best place to be alone because there was nothing to *do* at the beach. If she'd been tasked with counting the grains of sand, she couldn't have done it. If someone had told her to stop the tide rushing in and out, she would have to say no. Grace had no control over the waves, over the movement of the clouds, or fog, or birds. The tiny sideways rushing crabs ignored her entirely. It was the most reassuring place in the world.

Grace made her way over the low dunes to where the shore flattened. She found a large piece of driftwood to sit on. She kept her eyes on the horizon, right where the sea met the sky, and let handfuls of sand play through her fingers.

She'd lost everything now. Last year she would have said her sister and her acupuncture practice were the two most important things in the world to her, but now she didn't care about work. Without her sister, without *Tox* next to her, who cared?

How had it come to this so quickly? To ... love?

Staring at the horizon, Grace knew the word was right. *Love.* She loved him. She hadn't planned it and certainly hadn't wanted it, but Tox was the reason her heart sang, he was why her blood pounded. She wanted to watch him come home safely from a shift at work. She wanted him in her arms at night. All night long.

He wasn't perfect. Nothing said he was right for her. There were plenty of ways Tox could improve.

Sitting there on the beach, Grace couldn't think of one single way he could be better, though.

And Samantha ... her sister was everything. She was a wonderful, smart, kind woman who'd been through hardships and had bounced up from each one. Why couldn't Grace get over trying to fix her?

The problem was that Grace *did* know best sometimes. She did know when Samantha was about to lose it, to freak out over the wrong man, to chase after something that wasn't worthwhile. She knew when Samantha was about to fail.

In front of the waves, she saw her sister's face almost as clearly as if she'd been there. *"It's my life. Not yours. Mine."*

How, then, was she supposed to stop Sam from making mistakes?

A little boy dressed in blue overalls carrying a yellow balloon ran in front of Grace, cutting his way through the sand, his small feet kicking up sand behind him. It wasn't, of course, the boy from the pier who had almost lost his balloon, the one Tox had saved for him, but the boy reminded Grace of that moment.

The boy's mother, a young blond, chased after him, but

she was still a good city block behind. There was no harm the child could get into here unless he ran into the waves, and he was well away from the waterline. The mother looked relaxed. The child looked happy.

All Grace could see was the balloon. It wasn't tied around his wrist—he was just holding it. And he wasn't holding it tightly enough.

She launched herself to her feet and jumped forward. The boy's fingers loosened. "No!" Grace shouted! "Hold it! Tighter, hold it tighter!"

But even though Grace lunged forward as fast as she could, she couldn't grab the string in time. The balloon floated up, so brightly yellow against the clear blue sky.

The child burst into noisy tears, and the mother caught up. "What are you *doing?*"

"No," said Grace, holding out her hands. "Don't shout at him, he didn't mean to."

"I know he didn't. I'm shouting at *you*, not him. Why did you scare him like that?"

"I was trying to ..."

The woman picked the boy up and held him tight, brushing away the tears that came fast down his face. "Well, don't try."

All three of them looked up. The balloon was already tiny, bobbing in the wind high above.

"Thanks for nothing," said the woman.

Grace backed up and sat on the piece of driftwood with a thump. She listened to the boy wail in his mother's arms all the way down the beach.

Maybe Tox had a point.

She took out her cell phone and sent one short message to Samantha. "You're right. I promise not to fix things anymore. You're perfect the way you are."

CHAPTER 36

A week later, Grace paced in her driveway. It wouldn't work.

This couldn't possibly work.

Grace hoped it could make a difference, though. A start. Instead of the tin *nicho* she had on her wall where she held her hopes, this was another metal box, holding new hope. A red wagon, full of ice cream.

Samantha whistled when she saw it. "That's the most ice cream I've ever seen outside Skip's."

Grace nodded, taking a visual inventory, making sure she hadn't forgotten anything. Chocolate, strawberry, pecan praline, caramel swirl, vanilla, double chocolate fudge brownie, to start. That was the top layer of pints. Next to the ice cream were three jars of hot fudge, two of caramel and one butterscotch. She had four cans of whipped cream, and a large jar of maraschino cherries. She had paper bowls and plastic spoons.

Grace looked at her sister. "You should have seen Rose's face when I put all this on the check stand at the Mercantile. She thought I was kidding."

"What did you say? That you were having a party?"

"No, I just told her the truth, that it was crow, and that I was going to eat plenty of it."

"Come on, Grace. I know you didn't do or say anything that warrants this big an apology. What did you do? Punch the guy?"

"Not quite."

"Did you tell lies about his mother?"

Grace shook her head and grabbed the handle. "No. I tried to fix him."

"Oh," said Samantha simply. "I'm not sure you have enough ice cream."

"Want to come? I'm walking to his house."

"Are you kidding? Yeah. I'm going to hang out with Justin soon, but I can put him off."

Grace's heart stalled. "The guy who was driving that night you crashed?"

"Yeah." Her sister's voice held a delicate challenge, one that wobbled. Samantha was scared, too.

Grace wanted to say *No*. She wanted to say, *You can't. I won't let you.* But instead she said, "Of course. How's he doing?"

Samantha reached forward and threaded her arm through Grace's. "He's doing well." There was a pause, and the women walked toward the corner, the wagon making a clunking sound behind them.

"Good," Grace said. She meant it. Her sister got to make her own decisions. All of them.

"We're not dating," said Sam.

Grace kept her eyes on the stop sign in front of them. "You're not?"

"He's my sponsor. In AA."

"Oh." The breath left Grace's lungs. "Oh." She squeezed her sister's arm in hers.

The wagon rattled. A girl on a bike sped past, shouting something over her shoulder at the slower, smaller girl riding behind her.

"It would be okay if you dated him," said Grace.

Samantha just looked at her and smiled. "I know. I don't want to. But I do know that. And you know what?"

"What?"

"I'm glad you do, too."

In front of them, the sun was setting over the water. Twilight was dropping over Darling Bay like a crisp sheet. Fog rolled in swiftly. Another cool summer at the shore. And Grace was with her sister, on her way to Tox. There was no way her heart could hold more hope than it did now, at this exact moment.

## CHAPTER 37

It was nice having a dog to sit on his feet while he played cards with his friends, Tox thought. Everything might suck, and boy, did it ever, but poker and a dog did make things a little bit easier.

Of course, Lexie cheated at cards, and for one long second Tox thought about calling her on it. This was his man-cave, after all. His garage. No one cheated at cards at his favorite card table but him.

"What?" Lexie folded her legs underneath her on the orange chair. She was framed in front of the open garage door, and behind her, the sunset was scarlet streaks over palest blue.

"Yeah, what?" said Coin.

Tox narrowed his eyes. Hank said nothing and just raised. He usually raised.

"I don't trust you, woman," said Tox. "That's what."

Lexie laughed. Her lipstick was shining, and so were her eyes. Tox thought for a second about how Grace barely wore lip gloss. They were both beautiful women, but all Tox could think about was Grace.

He had to stop.

*Grace.*

"Queen's high," said Coin as he won the hand.

Lexie blew a *pfft* sound from between her teeth and then said, "See? Tox is right not to trust women. Dang Queen when I have the Jack …"

Coin leaned forward to collect his cash. "I trust women." He made an odd face in Lexie's direction. He almost looked as if …

Lexie didn't seem to notice.

Tox looked around the table in confusion. Was Coin trying to flirt with Lexie? Lexie from dispatch? That couldn't be right, could it? They were all friends here. They'd played poker off and on for more than five years now. Coin had a *kid* for Pete's sake.

"That's your problem," said Lexie. "Yours and Tox's. You trust women, and then they stomp on your heart. Although I need to point out to Tox that Grace is *my* friend, and therefore, I get to keep her and you can't be mad at me for her doing any stomping. Besides, I think you stomped each other."

Mad at Lexie for staying friends with Grace? Never. Tox looked down at his new hand of cards and realized he couldn't make heads or tails of it. He didn't know what was high or what was low. He couldn't tell what was red or what was black.

All he could see were Grace's amber eyes in front of him. Looking at him like he was something special. Looking at him like … almost like she loved him.

That would be something, because Tox loved her. He knew that, more deeply than he'd ever known anything else.

That was his whole problem, right there. He *loved* her. All of her, from that hair she barely fixed to those little ears that curled back so perfectly. From the adorable blush she got when he teased her to the heated flush she got when she was in his arms. From the way she stuttered slightly when she was mad to the way she thought she could fix the whole dang world.

Tox had to get over it. Over her. He wasn't good enough for her, and she knew it. She'd proven that by trying to fix him, and by the four aces in the deck in front of him, he wouldn't be fixed.

Tox wasn't good enough to warrant the tune-up.

Hank finally asked the question the other two hadn't dared to. "When you coming back to work, buddy?"

Tox shrugged. "You know."

Hank's mouth slid to the right, the way it did when he was thinking. Tox hated that face sometimes. "Nah. I don't know. How's your neck?"

"Good." Hurt like a son of a biscuit right now, actually, but Tox wasn't going to say that.

"How's your back?" asked Coin.

"Fine." It also hurt, but it was better.

"How's your head?" asked Lexie, leaning backward to grab a handful of chips from the card table behind her.

"Excuse me?"

"Chief said you had to get a psych."

Tox half-stood, knocking against the table so that everyone lurched for their beers. "HIPAA? No one's heard of that? Confidentiality?"

Lexie flapped a hand. "Oh, sue him, then. Make a pile of money and retire on medical."

Tox knew his jaw was hanging open.

"I'm *kidding*," said Lexie. "Jeesh. Besides, he said you took it on Friday and you passed."

Tox thumped back down into his seat. "Holy Helen."

Lexie lifted her shoulders and let them drop. "Dispatch knows everything."

Coin stopped staring at Lexie long enough to say, "Hey, are we expecting company?"

Up the driveway, through the open garage door, Tox saw Grace.

Pulling a wagon.

He felt like rubbing his eyes, but he knew what he saw.

It was the ice cream she was pulling behind her he didn't quite believe.

# CHAPTER 38

"Ice cream eating contest!"

Grace announced in as loud a voice as she could, which wasn't actually all that loud, given that she was staring at more people than she'd expected. And Tox.

Larger than life Tox.

He stood, and for one second, the sheer breadth of him reminded her of a comic book hero. She could almost see his cape.

"What?" he said, bringing Grace back down to earth.

She stuttered a little. "I-ice cream eating contest. I can eat more than you can."

Tox's eyebrows flew upward. At the card table, Lexie barked a laugh and took a handful of chips. Behind Grace, Samantha started to giggle.

"You what?" Tox's voice boomed.

"Are you up for the challenge?"

Tox took a step toward her and Grace longed, with all her heart, to close the gap between, to press her body against his, to let him know what was inside her heart.

Instead, she lamely held up an ice cream scooper and waggled it.

Her sister laughed harder. Oh, no. If Samantha was headed down the hysterical laughter trail...

"Bowl," Tox demanded. His face was perfectly still. Unreadable.

Grace handed him one and took one for herself. She opened the top of the caramel swirl with shaking fingers. This was such a *stupid* idea. Why had she thought it would be a cute way to apologize? She'd even thought it would be amusing to him, idiot that she was.

There was no smile cracking the sides of Tox's mouth.

"Hey!" said one of the other guys, the one with the deep black hair. "What about us?"

"Shut up, Coin," said Tox. He squatted so he could reach into the wagon.

"No! You can all have as much as you want. Help yourself." Grace had never felt more awkward in her life, hosting an impromptu dessert party in the middle of Tox's driveway.

Uninvited.

Unwanted.

She thought—again—about what she wanted to show Tox. That she didn't need to fix everything, that she could be as unhealthy as anyone else. As Tox put five scoops of ice cream, all different flavors, in his bowl, she realized this wasn't the way. This was just her trying to fix everything again.

Grace wanted to run.

Instead, she bent at the waist and kept adding flavors so that her number of scoops matched his. Six, then seven. Then she made sure her bowl held the same river of chocolate sauce, the same mighty peaks of whipped cream.

They stood straight. The sheer weight of ice cream in her bowl was making her arms heavy. She'd never be able to eat all this. Ever.

Coin reached between them for a bowl. "Lexie, what do you want?"

Lexie, who had been staring raptly as Tox and Grace battled for the maraschino cherries, said, "Don't worry about me. I'll get some in a bit."

"No, let me. Chocolate and vanilla, right?"

Lexie looked surprised. Grace wondered for the first time if Lexie had ever thought about having a romance at work. She'd have to ask her that the next time she saw her.

Now, though, it was time to eat.

Grace followed Tox onto the grass. They sat, cross-legged. Methyl leaned against Tox and tried to take licks out of his bowl. Sunset had settled now, and street lights were popping on with audible snaps. The sky to the west was still dark violet, and the air was heavy and damp with salt.

Grace normally loved this time of night.

It was too bad she was about to pass out from nerves. And from annoyance at Samantha still laughing in the middle of the driveway. Hank stood next to her sister, a wide grin on his face.

"Glad we have an audience," said Grace around the first spoonful.

"Can't take the pressure?" Tox had already polished off what must have been a whole scoop.

"Oh, I can." Grace took another bite, ignoring the brain-freeze. "I'm just concerned about you."

Tox's spoon slowed.

Deep green eyes met hers in the dim light. They said so much, in a language Grace was afraid she didn't speak well enough. Her breath caught.

Tox said quietly, only for her ears, "What are you trying to prove?"

Grace ate two more bites before she said, "That I don't have to fix you."

"You're saying I can eat ice cream whenever I want."

Grace felt despair flood through her like ice water. "It's dumb. It's so stupid. I can't believe I'm doing this."

Tox's eyes got even darker. "I like it."

"You do?"

"It's just that this can't work."

Grace's head dropped. "I know." She couldn't prove herself with cream and sugar.

"I'll never be the person you need me to be."

Her head lifted. "What?"

"I hurt people."

Dropping the bowl on the grass, heedless of the chocolate sauce soaking into his lawn, Grace pushed herself forward so that they sat, knee to knee. "What are you talking about?"

"It's all I've ever done. The Angel of Death. I bring destruction wherever I go, and I'm not doing that to you, too."

"No, no." She touched his forearm lightly. He tensed under her hand, as if she'd hit him. "You have that all wrong."

"You obviously haven't been paying attention, then. Did you know I don't even have a job right now?" He set his bowl on the grass and leaned backward, looking up through the acacia branches. "Not really. I'm on leave. If my back doesn't get right, if I don't pass the psych, I'm out for good. I've failed at the only thing worth doing. And I've failed the only woman worth ..."

Grace held her breath. He had to finish the sentence. He had to.

But he said nothing more. She watched the pulse under his chin where the dark stubble was thick.

Behind her, Samantha had finally stopped laughing, her hiccups fading away to nothing. Grace heard a muffled whisper and then shuffling. Then the garage closed with an old motor's whine.

They were alone on the grass, under the stars. Grace looked up, too, and saw one wink at her. Methyl licked her hand. The lick and the wink were the signs she needed.

They didn't help with her nerves at all, though. Her voice shook as she said, "What woman? How did you fail her?"

Tox brought his gaze back to hers. "You know exactly what I mean."

"You didn't fail me."

"I did. I do. Everyday."

"You have your inhaler on you?"

"What? Yeah. Of course." He scrabbled at his pocket. "Do you need it?"

"No. But you could save my life if I needed you to. But you know what?"

"What?" His voice was strained.

"I don't need you to. I have a good life. And you do, too. Let me be near you."

"What if I fail? I do that so often—I can't fail *you*."

Grace shrugged. "It's love. You take your chances."

"What about that matchbook of yours?"

"The one in my *nicho*?"

Tox touched her wrist lightly, as if he thought she might disappear. "Yeah. You were scared of being burned."

"I thought that, yeah. But I just realized something."

"What?"

Grace said carefully, "That's where I keep my hopes."

"Yeah?"

"Guess I was hoping for a firestarter."

Tox made a sound somewhere between a choke and a laugh. "I have a can of lighter fluid on the back porch if you need help with that. And it's Clement."

"What?"

"My first name is Clement."

Grace's heart melted faster than the ice cream in the grass. They were so close now. If she leaned her head in, she could rest her forehead on his. He smelled of chocolate and something darker, something all him. "I like that."

"You can call me that, then." He drew away an inch. "But only you. No one else."

"No one else," said Grace.

Tox kissed her then. In the kiss she could feel everything he was too scared to say, all the things she knew he'd tell her that night, when they were really alone, naked in his bed. He would tell her he wanted her to be there in the morning, and the morning after that. She would agree. There were so many things she felt on his lips, tasted on his tongue. But the most important thing, he said out loud.

"I love you," Tox said, his mouth on hers, his hand against her cheek. "Is that crazy? Because I do."

"Yeah, it's kind of crazy. And I love you, too." Grace grinned. Then she added, "Clement."

From inside the house, they heard Samantha's giggle drift out the open window. At their side, Methyl licked at the ice cream in the grass. And overhead, a star winked down on Darling Bay.

Dearest reader,

For quite a few years, I worked in the fire service as a 911 dispatcher. For the last five of those years, until I was able to quit and write full time, I worked and lived in the fire house on 48-hour shifts, napping in rotations when it was slow enough to do so.

No one knows better than me what firefighters are like (*insert cry-laughing emoji here*).

Are they all hot? Um, no. You should see them in the kitchen first thing, crowded around the coffee pots, pre-shower. They're animals.

But yes, some are sexy. Some are *damn* hot, you might have noticed.

And the thing they almost all have in common is their hearts of gold. They *do* want to save you from the fire, from the car accident, or like Tox, from all the bad stuff.

And in the next one? I got to write about Lexie, the dispatcher. I'm definitely *not* her, nor did I fall for a coworker (in real life, that's messier than it looks). But it was so much fun to let that dispatcher dream of love and then give it to her. I hope you love it! Turn the page for a quick sample!

    with love and my thanks,
    Rachael

PREVIEW OF BURN

Keep reading for a preview of the second book in The Fire-fighters of Darling Bay series, *Burn*!

Hope you love it!
Rachael

CHAPTER 1

The guy just wasn't getting it.

Lexie sighed and stepped on the pedal so her voice would carry to the firefighter who was on her last nerve. "2219 Ivy. Repeating. Two two one nine. Do you copy?"

Coin Keefe's voice filled her headset. "Copy two two one nine. There's still no one answering the door, and there's no key where you reported. Can you call back?"

"Affirm." Lexie knew she sounded short, but good grief, the call was for an eighty-two-year old woman who had fallen in her bathroom. She'd told him that. What, did Coin expect that the patient would get up and go unlock the door because they couldn't find the key under the pink flamingo? Coin probably just wanted her to say pink flamingo on the radio again. Firefighters always got a kick out of the dumbest things.

Okay, maybe everyone at the fire department did. Last week she'd gotten to say that a person had slipped on a banana peel. In nine years of working dispatch, she'd never heard of that happening in real life. All the guys who tromped through dispatch to see if she'd really said what they thought they'd heard hadn't heard of it, either. *No one* slipped and fell on a banana peel unless there was a laugh track attached. The victim, thankfully, was mostly unharmed.

The woman's voice was weaker on the phone now. "Hello?"

"I'm still here, ma'am. We're trying to get in to help you, but the key's been removed from your hiding place."

"Oh, no. I remember now. My nephew borrowed the key the last time he came over. Oh, dear."

"Is there another way in?"

"Around the back, the sliding glass door should be unlocked."

It wasn't surprising. In Darling Bay, most people left their back doors unlocked, if not their front ones as well. Officially, Lexie disapproved of this, if asked for her dispatcher opinion. Of course it wasn't safe. Crime happened, even in their small coastal town. But heck, it sure made the fire department's job easier.

Depressing the foot pedal so the firefighters—but not the patient—could hear her, she said, "Engine One, the back slider should be open."

"Copy."

"Ma'am," Lexie said to the woman, "I'm just going to keep you on the phone until they get in there, okay? I want to make sure you're all right."

"Honey, I told you, I'm not hurt. I just can't move."

A lot of elderly people thought this, until they tried to stand. Lexie hated that she took so many broken hip calls. Once the first hip went, many people lost their mobility, then their strength and their resistance to infection . . . "I know, but just stay on the line with me a little longer, do you mind doing that for me?"

"Just one strong young man should do it."

Lexie smiled. "Okay."

"Or two. I'm not a little person anymore. Two strong young men should do the trick to get me back on my feet."

"I understand. I'm not that little, either."

"Nothing wrong with that, honey. Can you just make sure you're sending me the good ones?"

"The good men?"

"I mean the handsome ones. I don't want the old ones. Oh, and I want men. Strong young men."

"I picked up on that."

"Do you even *have* any women working there?"

What an embarrassing question to be asked on a recorded line. "We do. We have three." In the whole department, consisting of almost seventy firefighters, only three were women. Women belonged in dispatch, and always had. Not on the fire line. Or at least that's the way the fire department in Darling Bay worked. It was a thing. Lexie hated it, but it was a thing.

"I don't want any women. Waste of time when I need help."

"They're very strong women," said Lexie.

"I'm sure they are. But they're not what I want. Once I called 911 and all I got was a huge man who looked as if he drank too much and a couple of whippersnappers who seemed scared of me. You best not be sending me that group again."

Lexie was having a hard time not laughing out loud now. That must have been Murphy's crew. He'd captained Engine One before retiring a few years back, and he'd been the training captain so he always had the new guys with him. Murphy *had* liked his whiskey on his nights off. And his beer, and his ouzo, and his bourbon …

"No, I made sure the handsome ones are coming, ma'am." It was true, actually. Tox was a big guy who struck women dumb as he walked past them while wearing his dark blue uniform. Lexie had seen it happen at Mabel's Cafe too many times to count. Coin, with his dark black hair and quiet confidence, was classically good-looking, Lexie supposed. Maybe almost movie-star good-looking. Reporters always liked to snap his picture, his face coated with soot, after fires. And Hank carried his height well and had a very sweet smile.

"Oh, good. Just the handsome strong young men. That's all I want." She made a content humming noise in Lexie's ear. Well, at least she wasn't the panicked type.

"They should be with you any minute. Do you hear them in the backyard yet?"

"I don't hear a thing, dearie. I can barely hear you."

Lexie pressed the foot-pedal. "Engine One, patient's still awaiting contact." That should get them to move a little faster.

There was a pause and then, over the radio, came a startled yip. Then Coin's voice, shouting. "Darling Fire, we're inside the residence. Get her to call off her dog!"

"Ma'am," said Lexie quickly. "Call your dog."

"What? I can't quite hear you."

Coin keyed up on the radio again but barking was the only thing that came across. Wild, frantic, angry barking.

"It's *really* important," said Lexie loudly, "that you *call off your dog.*"

"But I don't *have* a dog," wailed the woman. "Where are the strong young men?"

With a stomp, Lexie said on the radio, "Engine One, you're in the wrong house. Patient has no dog."

Tox came up on the radio, roaring over the barking, "Two two one nine?"

"Affirm," said Lexie crisply. "Ivy. Confirm you're on Ivy?"

A long pause.

Then Coin's voice came across the radio. "Darling Fire, we're on Oak. We copy Ivy. Switching locations."

Lexie flicked her mute switch so the woman wouldn't hear her sigh. Then she said, "Ma'am, those strong young men are almost with you. They're right around the corner, I promise."

## CHAPTER 2

Of course it had to be Lexie on the radio. Coin thumped the side of the driver's door of the engine with his fist after parking in the bay at Station One. It *would* have to be her, when he was busy screwing up. Looking back on his almost ten year career, almost every time he'd messed up on a call, she'd been on shift to listen to him being a dumb-ass. That made sense—they'd always been on A shift together, and the dispatchers had the same 48-hour schedule as the firefighters did. Two days on, four days off. Not too shabby.

And that's why Lexie had heard him screw up. Again.

In the day room, he heard a chorus of laughter.

"Woof!" hollered Luke. "Grrrr."

Guy Mazanti threw a stuffed dog at him.

Coin caught it one handed. "Really? Did you guys go out and spend money on this?" How had the truck even found time? They must have left the station as soon as they heard the call, because sure enough, the little old lady had just been a pick-up-put-back. No need to take her to the hospital. They'd only been out of the station a grand total of maybe thirty minutes. Forty-five if you counted the time spent at the house on Oak trying to repair the damage they'd done. And the truck crew had time to buy a stuffed dog to throw at him. "Very resourceful." He tucked the dog under his arm and pushed the day room's swinging door.

"Hey!" yelled Luke. "We were going to give that to Methyl!"

Methyl was Tox's yellow mutt and spent A-shift days at the station. She had her own crate, full of the stuffed animals she loved. Methyl didn't need another one. The stuffed dog was Coin's now.

And it was time to face the music in dispatch.

Sure enough, Lexie was sitting at her terminal, head propped on her fist, her eyes wide. Those boisterous red curls were piled on her head and she had tired smudges under her eyes, and she was still the prettiest girl in town. "Hoo boy. I can't *wait* to hear this."

He held out the stuffed dog. "Arf."

She smiled then. Grinned, really. "Is that for me?"

"Sure is." Let the truck guys tell her later they'd bought it. He didn't have to come clean about that.

"Adorable. Now spill. How did you mess that one up so good?"

Coin sighed and sat in the guest chair at the small round table. Telling her about it was a good excuse to be in dispatch, not that he ever tried very hard to find one. Coin just knew he wanted to be near her way more than he wanted to hang out with the guys down the hall. She was round and curvy in all the right places, and that rose tattoo of hers wound so enticingly out from the sleeve of her uniform polo. How many times had he wanted to ask to see the whole thing? Yeah, being in dispatch was better than listening to Tox try to train Methyl to sit for the millionth time. "You remember that fire we had last year on Ivy?"

"Oh, it was the same hundred block, right?" She turned and punched some keys, her fingers flying. "Yeah, it was right next to door to the patient tonight."

"I worked the back of that on the Charlie side."

Her grin got wider. "So you were on Oak for the fire. Not on Ivy."

He nodded. "And then apparently I drove right back to Oak when I heard Ivy."

"And Tox and Hank didn't notice."

"They're just dumb."

"No, they're not," said Lexie.

They weren't. They just hadn't noticed. It was his fault —Coin was the engineer. The driver. Sure, Tox was his captain and he was supposed to navigate, but in a town like Darling Bay, with only twenty thousand residents, they mostly knew exactly where they were going. His guys trusted him.

"Was anyone home?"

"In the house we broke into? Yeah."

Lexie laughed. "More. Don't you dare stop there."

"We had to break the side kitchen window in order to reach the latch for the sliding glass door."

"Because it was locked, even though I'd told you it was open, and you weren't wasting any more time on what silly dispatch said."

"Mmm." Coin didn't want to agree, but she was right. "So we bust in. This huge dog, massive, maybe a German Shepherd mixed with Malamute, rushed us."

"What did you do?"

"I threw a sandwich at him."

Lexie shook her head as if she thought she'd heard him wrong. "A sandwich."

"Yep."

"What kind?"

"Peanut butter, pickle, and grape jelly."

"Number one, that is disgusting and probably illegal in seven states, and number two, why did you have that in your pocket?"

"Serena came by earlier with her mother, and she'd made it special for me."

"Because she hates her father, obviously."

Coin knew Lexie was joking, but it still struck a small, quiet nerve. Serena loved him as any eleven-year-old girl loved her father. How long would it be until he could no longer say that? Soon she'd be in her teens and she'd hate him just like the child-rearing books said she would. It would break his heart when that happened. "Probably."

Lexie looked chagrined. "Coin, I'm sorry. I was kidding."

He pushed a knuckle into the tabletop. "I know. I'm just trying to prep myself for the teen years. You know I hated my father. I don't want the same thing to happen with my daughter and me."

"I never hated my father when I was a teenager."

"No one ever hated Robert Tindall." Coin had admired the district chief, though he'd only worked under him a year when he'd died. The whole town had grieved, but no one more than Lexie. She'd been on the radio when it had happened. A hoarder's house fire on Smythe Lane. An electrical line had come down and draped itself over the chief's rig while he was taking over incident command, but he hadn't known it was there. When he'd touched the back door to set up his mobile radio post, he'd been electrocuted almost instantly. The guys had worked him harder than anyone they'd ever worked, abandoning the empty house and letting it burn to the ground, but they never got a rhythm back.

Lexie had dispatched it all, refusing to let anyone take her radio that night. She'd come close to not being able to come back.

But Lexie was tough. So tough. Coin had thought that night that she was braver than any of the guys on the line. Her voice hadn't even shaken.

Now she said, "I was too busy hating my mother," and her eyes sparkled. "Still am, as a matter of fact. More, please, about the call. And that disgusting sandwich."

"The sandwich is a joke between Serena and me. I told her one day I'd make her a peanut butter, pickle, and jelly sandwich, just joking around, but Serena latched on to it as a thing, and now she actually likes them that way. I don't love them—"

"Because you're sane."

"—but she thinks I do, so she wraps them up tight in plastic wrap and sticks them in the pockets of my work pants sometimes. I'd just found it on the way to the call."

Lexie shook her head. "How do you not find a sandwich? In your pocket?"

"Cargo pockets. Do you know how much crap we keep in here?"

"So you're telling me you threw the sandwich in your pocket at a German Shepherd. That's kind of adorable."

Coin felt his face go red. He hated it when that happened in front of Lexie. Nothing worse than a man who blushed.

CHAPTER 3

There was really nothing cuter than a man who blushed, Lexie decided.

Sweet Coin.

"Oh, my gosh, I'm tired of sitting." She hit the button that raised the bank of monitors—the radio, the phone, the CAD—so that she could stand and work at the same time. At least Darling Bay Fire had sprung for a new ComCen when they'd redone the station five years back. It was a small room, full of computers—six screens at each of the four terminals—but with the big window and the raised ceiling, it felt spacious enough. On the center table was a collection of colored gourds—Sue's contribution—and in an early nod to Halloween, a plastic skull lit up and blinked next to the fax machine.

Lexie finished adjusting her work desk to the right height and leaned against it. "Okay. So who was in the house?"

"A man who was busy ignoring his dog. He didn't know we'd broken in until we went back, after picking up our patient. He just thought the dog had been barking at squirrels."

"Big squirrels in uniform carrying sandwiches."

"He was pretty heated. We had to do the board-up for him."

"You should have thrown your pickle at *him*." Lexie bit her bottom lip to keep from giggling. "So did the little old lady approve of the crew I sent her?"

Coin shot her a sideways look. "What exactly did you say to her?"

"She wanted the handsome ones."

Coin flexed his right arm. "Well, what can I say?"

"I told her Engine Two was out of quarters, but that I could send you guys."

"Liar," said Coin. "It was a Zone One call. And Tox is way better looking than Devo."

Lexie crossed her legs under herself. "Devo is hot. But you're better looking."

Coin coughed, and then said, "Stop it."

"It's true." Lexie tilted her head, taking a good, close look at Coin. He really could be in movies, with that hair so black it was almost blue and those dark chocolate eyes. He had heavy cheekbones and deliberate eyebrows. His jaw was firm, and he kept himself clean shaven, even going so far as to shave at night sometimes. The things she knew about these guys. "Why is your nose crooked?"

Coin touched the bridge of his nose. "Ummm."

"No! Don't get shy!" Coin was so quiet around some of the other dispatchers they called him Ghost behind his back. They'd see him in the hallways, and then he'd be gone, as silently as he'd come. "You're not allowed to do that with me. We're friends. Besides, your nose gives you a ..."

"A ridiculous look?"

"A look of badness."

Shaking his head, Coin said, "No idea what you're talking about."

"Like you broke it in a bar fight or something. Like you did something that gave you a bad reputation."

"I can't believe you don't know how I did it."

How had she never asked? He was her best friend, the person she talked most to. Lexie leaned forward in eagerness, drawing herself closer to him by pulling her chair along her workspace tabletop. "Tell me you dropped your Harley at ninety on a blind curve at night. Maybe while you were outrunning the cops."

"Nope. Nothing that fast. In fact, I was standing still at the time."

"You warded off a robber who clocked you before you decked him, and then you returned the old lady's purse while blood ran down your chin."

Coin's eyes widened. "You're gory, huh?"

"I like to imagine things."

Rolling his chair a foot forward, Coin looked over his shoulder. In a lower voice, he said, "I was on a call. On the ladder, thirty feet up."

"This happened at work?" Why didn't she remember that?

"I was a rookie. I don't think you had started yet. Anyway, it was dark. It was storming. Lightning crashed overhead."

"Lightning and you were on a ladder? No bueno. Were you *hit*?"

"I was."

Lexie couldn't stop the little screech she gave. The business line rang and she made short order of it, transferring the citizen to the voice mail they wanted. Then she said, "Go on."

"Like I was saying, I was hit."

"You could have been *killed*. Lightning actually hit you?"

"Now, now," Coin spread his fingers wide. "Slow your ponies. I didn't say what hit me."

"You're killing me."

"I was hit by a falling branch."

Lexie blinked hard. "You were up in a tree?"

One nod. "I was. On a very important call."

"Cat in a tree. You broke your nose on a *cat in a tree call*? How is it even possible that I've never heard this before?"

"I pay the guys cash once a month not to bring it up."

Lexie laughed. "I almost believe you. Did you get the cat?"

"Nah. Branch hit me in the face, I stuck to the ladder like a burr, which your dad liked, when he heard about it."

"I bet he did. He liked stubborn."

"Once I was on the ground and bleeding everywhere, Tox told the lady who called that she and her kitten could stay up the tree till Christmas, and we weren't coming back."

"And now you hate cats, like every other man. Except you have a reason."

Coin rubbed his nose. "Truth?"

"Duh."

"I went back and got the kitten after I got off work. I climbed the tree and put it in my shirt and climbed down. Scratched my shirt to ribbons and I was bleeding when I put my feet on solid ground."

Lexie clapped her hands. "I am so mad that I've never heard this."

"No one knows that part. I don't even know why I'm telling you."

"Because you adore me." She knew she was Coin's favorite dispatcher, and he was by far her favorite firefighter, though she loved all her guys. "What did the woman say when you showed up with her kitten?"

He sighed, and the tops of his cheeks got that wind-burned look again. "Turned out it wasn't hers. She'd just heard it crying up there. She didn't even like cats."

"What did you do with it?"

He shrugged. "You know."

Lexie gasped. "You still have it." She waited for a second to read his face. "You *do*. Coin Keefe, that is the cutest story I've ever heard."

"Serena wanted a kitten."

"Do not *lie* to me. She's eleven. Your wife—"

"Ex-wife," Coin said.

"Your ex-wife was probably barely even pregnant back then. And don't tell me Janice wanted to keep it because I know her, too, don't forget. It's not like she's the warm and cuddly type."

"I will admit," Coin said, "that I wanted to keep the cat. So I did."

Lexie rested her chin on her fists again. "What did you name it?"

Coin sighed. "Nosey."

"Come on, tell me."

"That's its name."

"Oh!"

Coin rubbed his nose again self-consciously.

Lexie bent forward at the waist laughing. Sometimes

she was self-conscious about how loud her laugh was, but her big laugh always made Coin laugh, too, and this time was no exception.

"I'm sorry," she wheezed after she'd grabbed her breath back, "but that's seriously the best name. You are the cutest guy ever."

Coin groaned. "Great."

"Why do you say it like that? You're adorable."

"No firefighter wants to be adorable." He glared at Lexie, a dark, brooding glare that she didn't buy for a minute.

"That's how you get all the action, right?"

He goggled at her. "Are you kidding me?"

"You nag 'em with your adorability."

"I *wish* you would stop saying that."

"Why do girls go out with you, then?"

Coin stood. "This has been fun. I'm going to go see how Luke's getting on with dinner."

"Don't you go anywhere, Keefe." Lexie felt a stirring of excitement. "I'm suddenly intrigued by your recent dating history. Why don't you ever tell me about it? Sit."

"You don't tell me what to do." He said it with a small grin. They both knew she did tell him what to do. That was her job, after all.

"Sit? Please?" Niceness wouldn't hurt, she supposed. "I'll make some coffee for you."

"You make it too weak."

"I'll make it so that you can't stir it at all."

"Sounding better," he granted, hovering next to the chair he'd just vacated.

"So that the fork melts when you put it in the cup."

He sat. "Why would you put a fork in a cup of coffee?"

"You ask too many questions," said Lexie, filling the

small carafe at the water cooler. "I get to ask to the questions. I'm the dispatcher. I'm the one who grills you."

Coin raked his fingers through his dark hair. "I'm getting a little worried."

"You should be." She added five scoops of coffee instead of her normal two for the half-sized carafe and pushed start.

Engine Three radioed, "Three in quarters."

Lexie pushed the headset transmit button that was hooked at her hip. "Darling copies."

"It weirds me out when you do that," said Coin.

"What?"

"I can't hear anyone talking and then you respond."

She tapped the headset she kept on when she was in the ComCen. "I love the wireless."

"If it means you make me coffee while still working, I love it, too."

Lexie leaned again on her console and rubbed her hands together. "Okay. Tell me about the last girl you dated."

"You met her."

"No, I didn't." Lexie would remember. She popped a Tootsie Roll into her mouth. "Want one?"

He shook his head. "You did meet her. At the Christmas party."

"You didn't take anyone last year." Instead, Lexie remembered him dancing with all the dispatchers, one by one, while the other guys danced with their girlfriends and wives. He hadn't asked Lexie. She'd wondered if she just wasn't his type—maybe he liked the skinny ones.

Now was her time to find out.

"Monica," Coin said. "The vet assistant."

"Oh! The one you brought like three years ago?" That couldn't have been his last girlfriend.

He cast a look out the window behind her. "That's her."

Lexie spoke around the candy. "She was so *boring*."

"Really, Lex? Thanks."

She put a hand over her mouth. "Sorry. But she talked about her cat, like, the entire night."

"She and I had that in common. Cat-lovin'."

"See?" said Lexie triumphantly. "You're adorable."

Coin fixed her with a stare that suddenly made Lexie want to take back the word. He didn't look adorable. For one moment, Coin smoldered.

Lexie choked on her Tootsie Roll.

# CHAPTER 4

Lexie managed to pull in a breath deep enough to cough. The Tootsie Roll dislodged from her esophagus.

"Do you need the Heimlich?" Coin was already next to her, his face serious.

She tried to laugh and ended up coughing harder. "No," she managed.

"Put your hands to your neck in the universal choking symbol if you do."

Lexie nodded. Sweat broke at her hairline. Was it the Tootsie Roll or him being so close that was making her so nervous? Her skin felt superheated, and she flipped on her desk fan.

Coin laid his hand on her back and rubbed firmly in a circle. "You all right?"

Had he ever touched her before, besides maybe a brief hug when they got together with the guys for poker? Lexie said, "Fine." She turned her chair so he wasn't touching her.

Time to take back the conversation. "What dating site are you on?" she squeaked.

"Losers-R-Us dot com."

"You're not on *any* dating sites?" That couldn't be true, could it? A guy like him would be swamped online. He'd have a hundred girls to choose from in twenty-four hours, even in a town as small as Darling Bay.

"Are you on one?"

She cleared her throat again. "Of course."

Coin stared at her. "You go on dates with total strangers."

"It's fun." That was her party line. Lexie tried very hard to believe it. She even succeeded some of the time.

"It's fun to go on blind dates and make small talk with people you have nothing in common with?"

Rescue Two gave an almost indecipherable squawk on the radio, but Lexie know Danny's mumbles well. "Copy," she said. "Rescue Two available on the air." Dating *could* be fun. Sometimes. In the last year, though, she'd only had a couple of okay dates with guys who turned out to be too boring to see twice. "People are fascinating."

"Tell me your most fascinating date."

She took a moment to think. "Last year, there was the guy who was a commercial fisherman."

"Why?"

"Why what?"

Coin's tone was pushy now. "Why was he fascinating?"

She'd been fascinated by his thick wrists. She'd stared at them all night, looking at the way the veins on the backs of his hands bulged, wondering if he was ... well-endowed everywhere. She hadn't found out, though. He'd called her, yeah. But she hadn't gone out with him after that one night.

But it hadn't only been his wrists that had fascinated her. "Because his job was so dangerous."

"Pulling salmon out of the ocean?"

She shot him the look that quieted most battalion chiefs. "It has a higher fatality rate than firefighting. Fishing as a profession has *the* highest fatality rate in America. By far." It was why she'd accepted his offer of a date.

"Oh." Coin looked nonplussed for a moment, then he recovered. "So you can meet amazing people online. Why are we talking about this again?"

Lexie twisted so she could reach her personal computer. "We're putting you online right now."

"That, my friend, would be a cold day in a very deep place I hope never to visit." He leaned back in his chair and laced his fingers behind his head.

Lexie lifted her phone. "Don't move."

"What?"

She snapped his picture. "And *that* is going to be your profile picture."

"What do I get out of this?"

Raising an eyebrow, Lexie said, "This is a conversation you usually have with a parent. But if you need me to explain it to you ..."

"Quit it," said Coin. "I mean it. I'm happy the way I am."

"Alone."

"I have Serena."

"Alone half the time."

"I call it single. Not alone."

"Coin, I'm single. Being single means going out with people. With friends. On dates. Doing things that are fun and frivolous and sometimes ridiculous and having a good time doing them."

He stood and got himself a cup of the coffee that had stopped sputtering into the carafe behind him.

"You don't do that," continued Lexie. "The nights you don't have Serena, what do you do?"

"Work overtime so I can keep paying Janice."

"And *that's* what I'm saying. Come on," she said, bringing up HoldMe.com. "Let me do this for you."

"So tell me," said Coin, leaning against the counter and taking a big sip of the coffee Lexie knew was probably still too hot. "What are you getting out of this?"

"Nothing but the pure, unadulterated joy of helping another human being."

"Screw that," he scoffed. "Not good enough."

"What would make it worth it for you? I'll write the ad for you, if you want."

"Nah," he said, taking another sip. "You'll have to do that anyway, since I know I'm not going to. Something else. Something better."

Lexie didn't know what he meant. "What else can I do to talk you into it?"

"A bet."

Lexie squinted at him. "I don't gamble."

"What about our poker games?"

She grinned. "That's not gambling. That's taking candy from babies. And besides, I don't trust you. What do you mean by bet?"

"A bet means we're both into this. That we're both invested. I have no interest in just being your entertainment, something for you to laugh at."

What if his feelings were hurt because she was trying to get him online? "You know I'm not teasing you. I'm pushing you because I care about you."

"Then prove it."

"How?"

"Put something on the line. Something that matters to you."

Something that mattered to Lexie? What *didn't* matter to her? Everything did. Coworkers' problems, and citizens' complaints. 911 calls mattered almost as much as the little old lady who needed help opening her garage door. Friendship mattered to Lexie. Family did, too, even though she tried to pretend sometimes she didn't have a mother.

Love mattered to Lexie. Since she and her last boyfriend—a tax accountant who had loved spending time with his online game more than he had with her—had broken up last year, though, she had tried not to think about that too hard.

"What?" Coin said, his voice demanding. "You thought of something."

"No ..."

"What?"

"It's too hard to ..."

"Just tell me."

Lexie felt her skin heating again. "Love."

"Love?" Coin's eyebrows flew upward. "From a website?"

"You asked what mattered," said Lexie, embarrassed. But she meant it. It was important. "Love matters."

"Love it is, then." Nodding emphatically, Coin said, "Love is our bet."

"How do you make a bet on love?"

He held up a finger. "One, we tell the truth. Promise?"

Lexie nodded once. Truth was easy. She often got in trouble for telling too much of it, and she didn't think she'd lied to Coin even once.

"And two, we *try* to fall in love."

Lexie rolled her chair a few inches closer to him. "How do we do that?" she asked.

"If I have to tell you how to fall in love, sugar ..." he drawled.

She caught his scent—not the normal Axe body wash that so many of the guys on the line preferred. He smelled clean, like he'd just taken a shower. Like soap and shampoo, and something darker, a little smoky. Old fire scents caught in his clothing, maybe? Lexie felt something jump in her stomach. "A challenge. Okay, then. You know I *do* like a challenge."

"Yep," he said. "The last person to fall in love has to ..."

"Buy they other person dinner," said Lexie triumphantly.

"Are you serious? We're talking about changing our lives permanently, drawing other people into this game, and you think buying dinner will do it? No way. Go bigger."

"True," she said. "Okay. Bigger. Okay, the second person to fall in love has to buy the first one ... an *expensive* dinner for two, for the winner and his or her new squeeze. At La Spezia."

Coin groaned. "Bigger. What about a trip?"

"Ooh!" This was something she could get behind. "Where? Reno? Tahoe?"

"Hawaii."

Lexie was impressed but didn't want to show it. "Why stop there? Why not Tahiti? Or ..." She brought up the website she'd been looking at earlier. "Check this out. Bora Bora."

The picture she showed him was of idyllic thatched roof huts, staggered along joined piers. Each hut sat above crystal blue water. It looked like Lexie thought heaven should, if she got to talk to God about it.

"That." Coin pointed at the screen. "If you fall in love first, I'll buy you and your guy two round-trip tickets to Bora Bora."

"But that's so expensive!"

"What?" he said. "This is your idea. Besides, you're single, no kids, and you work overtime, just like me. You have the money."

What would have sounded rude anywhere else just came out as blunt. It was true. Most of them in the department worked too much, and money just kind of stacked up in the bank. Lexie wasn't great at spending it on herself, so her savings got bigger every year. Definitely a perk of the job.

Lexie narrowed her eyes. "But do *you* want to go to Bora Bora? Really? Because I can see you throwing the whole bet just to prove your point. You'll let me fall in love, and then send me and my ridiculously cute boyfriend away to the islands."

"You think I'm that generous?"

"Yes." One year, Lexie had run the Adopt-a-Family for Christmas, an annual tradition at the fire house. For one needy family the entire department had raised almost seven thousand dollars' worth of gifts. Then Coin's money had come in. He'd tried to make it anonymous, but the computer transaction had let his name slip through. He'd more than doubled the amount raised, and the family had been able to buy a used van with his funds. Lexie was the only one who knew. She hadn't run the program in subsequent years, but every year, she knew that something similar happened, moneywise. She had her suspicions.

"And what am I supposed to do if *I* win? Take Serena with me on the days I'm supposed to have her? Janice never lets me get out of a single one of my days."

"Have you ever, even once, *wanted* to get out of a day with your daughter?"

Coin had the grace to look chagrined. "No. But I know if I did, Janice would throw a fit and say she had an out-of-town business trip or something.

"I'll babysit, then."

"You?"

"Hey! What's wrong with me? I find your surprise offensive, my friend. And Serena's my little pal."

Coin drained his coffee cup and thumped it on the table. "When was the last time you babysat?"

Lexie stuck out her tongue at him.

"When?"

"I am a superb babysitter. I got an award for it once."

"How old were you?"

She'd been thirteen, and it had been an automatic award, given by 4H for completing the babysitting class. "Old enough."

"So you haven't watched a kid since you were a teenager." Coin grabbed a mug from under the microwave and poured her a cup. Without asking, he added cream.

"Thank you. How do you always know what I need?"

"Just because you're too stubborn to ask for anyone's help doesn't mean I can't read you like a book," said Coin.

"Hey, by the way, if she chokes on anything, I'm shockingly familiar with how to dial 911."

"Is that supposed to make me feel better?"

"What if I tell you I give CPR instructions all the time?"

"I am never, ever leaving my kid alone with you."

Lexie grinned. "Seriously. We could do this."

"Fall in love?"

For one long moment, Coin's dark gaze met hers. He

held her eyes for one second too long, and Lexie felt that strange thump echoing in the pit of her stomach again.

"Yeah. We could." Then she clarified, "Find someone to love. We could do that."

"Why don't you just go out with me, and we can cut out the middle part?"

She stared at him.

Then she laughed. "Oh, cut it out. For a second I thought you were serious."

There was a pause before he laughed, too. "A race to love," he said. "This is the most stupid plan we've ever come up with."

Lexie felt that hollow thump again and decided she was just hungry. "Agreed," she said. "Now. What's your profile name going to be?"

# KEEP READING!

Keep reading by grabbing *Burn* now! Just go to RachaelHerronBook.com to get your copy!

(Psst - there are special discounts over there, too!)

## ABOUT RACHAEL

**Rachael Herron** is the internationally bestselling author of more than twenty books, including thriller (under R.H. Herron), mainstream fiction, romance, memoir, and nonfiction about writing. She received her MFA in writing from Mills College, Oakland, and she teaches writing extension workshops at both UC Berkeley and Stanford. She's a New Zealand citizen as well as an American.

She'd *love* to hear from you! Sign up for her mailing list at RachaelHerron.com/Subscribe, then drop her a line and she'll write you back! (Seriously. She loves to hear from readers.) Plus you'll get a free short love story that will melt your heart, instantly! Or find her on social media!

instagram.com/rachaelherron

patreon.com/rachael

facebook.com/Rachael.Herron.Author

bookbub.com/authors/rachael-herron

youtube.com/@RachaelHerronWrites

www.ingramcontent.com/pod-product-compliance
Lightning Source LLC
Chambersburg PA
CBHW061433210726
48287CB00007B/2202